This Idea Will Work!

30/1794L

This Idea Will Work!

136 Ways to Revitalize Your Music Ministry

Work smarter!

Inspire and challenge your choir!

Invigorate your choral program!

by Bob Burroughs

Editor: Kris Kropff

Typesetter: Gregg Sewell

Cover Design: Melissa Dooley

Lorenz Publishing Company
A division of The Lorenz Corporation
P.O. Box 802
Dayton, OH 45401-0802

www.lorenz.com

Printed in the United States of America

ISBN: 0-89328-155-7

Foreword

There is a world of ideas out "there" in both church and school settings: good, solid ideas that offer opportunities for creative thinking, personal challenge, and inspiration; suggestions to make things happier in rehearsal and performance; and ways to do things better and easier and to help you work smarter.

With over 45 years of practical experience in the local church, as a college professor, and as the Director of the Church Music Department of the Florida Baptist Convention, most of the ideas in this volume have come through practical, hands-on experience. It has been my desire for some time to pass along these workable and usable ideas to a new generation of music ministers or college professors, as well as to seasoned men and women in places of music ministry who may be in need of a fresh, new idea or two. Many of these ideas come from three and a half years of Monday Morning Email, that went to some 1400-plus readers. As you read through these ideas, mark those that might be helpful to you. You'll be glad you did!

From my heart to yours, these ideas will work!

— Bob Burroughs

Contents

FELLOWSHIP AND MINISTRY

CHOIR OFFICERS AND THEIR RESPONSIBILITIES

CHOIR MEMBERS

WORSHIP AND WORSHIP PLANNING

TECHNOLOGY

Rehearsals and Director's Preparation

1 BEFORE THE REHEARSAL

Here are some suggestions that may make rehearsals a bit more interesting and exciting for your choir or ensemble.

A
Have all the proper music in the choir folder.

B
Have the choir room a comfortable temperature, even a bit chilly. It will warm up!

C
Make sure everyone has his or her own copy of each piece.

D
See that the room is clean, the chairs are straight and in place, and the evening's order or agenda is on the board. If there isn't a board, get one!

E
If you have a weekly choir newsletter or info sheet, put it in the folder slot or on each member's chair.

2 DURING THE REHEARSAL

Don't make any announcements in the choir rehearsal; put your newsletter to work, and let it take care of all such details. Teach your people to read the material!

If you don't use a weekly newsletter or information sheet, allow the choir president (you do have choir officers, don't you?) to handle the last part of each rehearsal, using part of the time to emphasize all announcements.

MORE

Work fast, work hard, and keep the choir busy at all times. Don't allow any time for whispering, jokes, or conversations. The highest compliment you can be paid as a conductor is: "You didn't give us any time to talk tonight!" Always stay ahead of the choir!

When finished with the rehearsal, quit – even if it is not 9:00 p.m.! Turn the rehearsal over to your president and go sit down. Let the choir president finish the time with prayer requests, a devotional thought, any major announcements, and a prayer.

Begin on time, every time, and end on time, every time! This is a very important point. It's just not fair for the rehearsal to begin ten minutes late because you're waiting on five or seven key people to arrive. If there are choir members in the room, go to work.

Begin rehearsal with something familiar, in a nice low register, so as to warm up the voice gently while still teaching and working on choral tone.

Rehearsals that are consistently

- stimulating
- refreshing
- interesting
- humorous
- innovative
- challenging
- exciting
- spiritually beneficial
- and not boring

will entice the choir members to attend consistently, for fear that if they miss even a rehearsal, they may miss something really great. Build this spirit in the choir and it will work for you.

3 A TONGUE-IN-CHEEK PRAYER FOR TODAY

Dear Lord,

Help me to relax about insignificant details beginning tomorrow at 7:41:23 am, EST. Help me to consider people's feelings, even if most of them are over sensitive. Help me to take responsibility for my own actions, even though they are usually not my fault. Help me to not try to run everything, but if you need some help, please feel free to ask me!

Help me to be more laid back, and help me to do it exactly right. Help me to take things more seriously – especially laughter, parties, and dancing. I ask for patience, and I mean right now! And help me not be a perfectionist (did I spell that correctly?).

Help me to keep my mind on one th – Look! a bird – ing at a time.

Help me to do only what I can do, and trust you for the rest. And would you mind putting that in writing? Keep me open to others' ideas, incorrect though they may be. Allow me to be less independent, but let me do it my way. Allow me to follow established procedures today. On second thought, I'll settle for a few minutes. And finally, I ask You to help me slow down andnotrushthroughwhatIdo. Amen.

4 ATTITUDE DETERMINES SUCCESS

Your attitude will determine the success or failure of your rehearsal – believe it or not! If you are happy, jovial, smiling, anxious and determined, rehearsal will go better. If you come into rehearsal carrying extra baggage, such as personal or family problems or staff strife, and are up-tight and stressed, it will have a major impact on those who attend the rehearsal, as well as on the one who conducts the rehearsal. Therefore, it is absolutely imperative that you rid yourself of as much stress as possible so that you can inspire, challenge and encourage your choir members to be better musicians and better Christians.

Side remarks, personal jokes and inappropriate humor are all out of place in a good and positive choir rehearsal. Keep your personal feelings to yourself and strive to challenge your people to be better musicians than they are. And under your direction, they will be if you prepare your rehearsal plan free of personal stress. Don't carry personal baggage into the rehearsal! Enjoy your people, love them, challenge them, encourage them, and stretch them to be better than they think they can be.

You can do it...with the right attitude!

5 CHECK-UP TIME *by David Smith, head of Knowledge Development at Unilever*

Here are some symptoms of an organization or program that is sick, or certainly not feeling well:

There is a tendency for repeated mistakes

There is duplicated work

Relationships are beginning to be strained

Good ideas seem to die on the vine

You can't keep up with your peers

You find yourself becoming too dependent on key individuals

You are too slow to launch new projects, programs or plans

If your program has any of these symptoms, perhaps a 'check-up' is due. Remember, a leader is not supposed to do everything by him or herself.

6 CONDUCTING

by Warren Fields, a dear friend who has retired from active music ministry but who knew the value of good conducting

I have learned a great deal about conducting from excellent teachers and have learned a few things through practical experience. Conductors tend to develop some mannerisms they should try to overcome. In my judgment, the mannerism that produces the most negative results is moving the mouth (audibly or inaudibly) either in rehearsal or in performance. There is probably no mannerism that is more detrimental to the overall choral performance. Believe me, you will be both surprised and pleased beyond words (no pun intended) if you will conquer the habit of singing with your choir or forming the words of the text with your mouth. The tenors don't really need you!!

Let me give some reasons:

1 You will be able to hear the choral parts and accompaniment more effectively if you conduct with your hands and arms and not your mouth. Listening carefully to your choir can become an art and you will be more sensitive to difficult spots than ever before because you will hear the errors and will be able to correct them!

2 You will have a greater variety of gestures at your disposal in the use of hands, facial expression and overall body language. When you move your mouth, the eyes of the singers will be fixed there and movements, therefore, have almost no meaning at all.

3 Your singers will begin to have more confidence in their own musical abilities, which will result in a better choral sound.

4 You will convey to the singers that you have confidence in your skills as a conductor — without the use of your mouth.

I have always wondered why conductors tend to 'mouth' the words, particularly when the singers have the music in front of them! We must sure look funny to them!

7 DREAM AT LEAST ONCE A DAY

When I was young in music ministry, serving First Baptist Church, Abilene, Texas, Dr. Phil Simpson, Organ Professor, Hardin-Simmons University and organist at the church, came to my office one day, sat down and watched as I was busily engaged in a multitude of activities. Finally, in a quiet voice, **he said these words to me,** which I will never forget:

"Bob…when do you ever sit and dream?"

"What do you mean?" I asked.

He said, "Bob…every creative person should put their feet up on their desk at least once a day and dream a dream, come up with a new idea, or think of how to do something differently to improve the ministry."

I had never thought about that concept.

I began to do just that. I was amazed at the creativity God poured into my life! That became a pattern for me each day, and I have continued that practice almost every day of my ministry. If you will take the time to be quiet, rest in Him, say scriptures over and over in your mind, and pray and think, God will pour into your mind new thoughts, concepts, dreams and visions for the future of your ministry. It will take time, but I encourage you to do this. You *will* discover a freshness in your ministry.

8 ENERGY

Energy is one of the keys to success with your choir, orchestra, and congregation. It is also the one thing that cannot be taught in school – it must be experienced!

People will give back to you 50% to 80% of the energy given to them by the leader. So, in any rehearsal, if the director feels bad and sluggish and only gives 90% of him or herself that evening, the group can be expected to give back some 45% to 80% of themselves in return.

Energy will make rehearsals fun and worth their attendance.

Here are some common sense things to help you get energy:

FOODS
Put into your body the things that will produce a high energy for you. Fruit is a wonderful energy food.

PROPER REST
Essential to a high energy level, especially on those rehearsal days. One can't go hard all day at work and at home and expect to have anything left that is fresh for rehearsal that evening. Take some time during that rehearsal day to relax a bit before going full force into the rehearsal situation.

SPIRITUAL STRENGTH
If your spiritual life is creative and innovative, and if your walk with God is regular and communication is open and free, you will have a new, abounding energy in life itself!

ATTITUDE
One of the most important items to boost your energy level. Your rehearsal attitude must be so intense that you purposefully avoid any conflicts prior to that sacred hour and don't waste your time in confrontation, but rather, save it for the rehearsal.

EXERCISE
Daily and consistent exercise such as walking, biking, free weights, LifeCycle, tennis, and more. Just do it!

The energy you spend in preparation for regular rehearsals will come back to you through the energy your choir gives back to you in response.

9 EVALUATE YOUR REHEARSAL WEEKLY

The conductor has the sole responsibility for a successful rehearsal. If it falls apart, if it is terrible, if it has no drive or sparkle, or if it is absolutely glorious, the conductor must accept full responsibility! Personal evaluation sometimes helps put rehearsal in a good perspective. Here are some good rehearsal-evaluation questions for your consideration:

Why was the rehearsal bad? good?	What factors contributed most to the failure or success?	Did the conductor have total control of the time or was it taken from him or her by talking, laughter, or jokes?	If so, what can be done to prevent this from happening again?	How was rehearsal paced?
Was there too much new music? too much old?	Was it one section or person causing the problems?	Was valuable time wasted while unimportant things happened, such as passing out music or working with the pianist?	Did you start – and end – on time?	Were you positive, upbeat, and gentle in your approach?

Try to have a rehearsal plan and follow it well. You may stray from it occasionally, but for the most part, the plan will keep you on a good track!

Rehearsal success, or failure,
is the sole responsibility of the conductor!

10 EVERYONE DESERVES TO HAVE THEIR OWN MUSIC

Nothing is more frustrating than to have an anthem in rehearsal, mark it as the conductor requests (in your own voice part, of course) and then have to pass in that score or place it on a table with all the other scores following rehearsal!

Consider allowing all of the choir members to keep their own scores, with all their own markings, and provide them with a packet or a three-ring binder in which to do so. This way the music in which they mark this week will be in their own music next week! This will pay great dividends to the conductor, and the performance! Trust me here!

11 FALL CHOIR/INSTRUMENTAL ENROLLMENT CELEBRATION

After you have promoted, re-promoted, and promoted again Choir/Instrumental Enrollment, The New Choir Year, New Beginnings, or whatever you call this period, it is now time to put your money where your mouth is! It is time to make the first rehearsal of the new season the very best in history, both to whet the appetites of those who are regular members and come faithfully and to interest those new people who will visit your rehearsal on that special, promoted, and publicized night! So:

See that the choir room looks really clean – floors swept, furniture polished, walls bright, all nonessential stuff removed. Make it look inviting.

Have the chairs 6-10 inches apart, if possible, so as not to be crowded.

Have the room cool, about 68 degrees. Remember: it will warm up.

Have balloons and streamers everywhere. Make the room festive.

Have the Fall music packet available to both new and old members, with everything in each one. No one should be without all of the music.

Have the music to be rehearsed either on a board or in the choir newsletter so the choir members can get their music in the right order.

Be sure to assign persons to care for visitors, to help them to 'know what to do'! Choir rooms can be, and usually are, very intimidating, especially for a first-time visitor! The person assigned should have a knowledge of 'what goes on' so as to lead the new person through the rehearsal, and allow them to be comfortable in a very uncomfortable setting.

Begin on time.

Make sure you are prepared and ready to take the singers or instrumentalists through their paces. Know your stuff!

Don't talk a lot! Don't give them dates and information that are 'way out there'. The choir members don't care to know what the Christmas music will be in 2005, even if John Rutter himself is going to make a personal appearance at your performance! Give them only the information they need to know for this week, and maybe next.

If possible, allow the choir officers to dispense information so as to get you out of the limelight.

Be humorous, be funny, be serious, be good, be musical, be competent, be their music minister. Don't sing. Listen carefully to the choir. You'll find more problems to fix if you listen!

Before choir time is over, compliment them on their good work and invite them to some very excellent refreshments, wherever you are allowed to have such!

Quit on time.

Be sure to personally greet each new visitor, and each returning choir member, yourself, one-on-one.

The following day, send post cards or a personal letter to everyone expressing your gratitude for the excellent rehearsal and how much you are looking forward to next week's rehearsal. (Remember: don't mention Christmas 2005 - they don't care!)

There you have it. A recipe for a successful Fall Choir/Instrumental Kickoff! Let me know if it works!

12 FALL IS UPON US; ARE YOU READY?

Whether you begin Fall rehearsals in August or wait till the Wednesday after Labor Day, the time is either here now, or approaching fast! Are you ready? Here are some questions that might help your thought process for Fall:

1
Are things in order?

2
Is the rehearsal room clean?

3
Are the robes clean?

4
Are the music packets full of the Fall/Christmas music?

5
Are the rehearsal chairs in good shape?

6
Is the coffee machine ready – new filters, sugar, sugar substitute, cream, spoons, napkins, cups, coffee?

7
Has music been chosen carefully to fit the sermon subjects for the Fall (if you are fortunate enough to have them)?

8
Has the music been ordered for Fall?

9
Is there a wide variety of music selected that will appeal to the wide variety of church members in your congregation as well as to the vast array of musical opinions in your choir or instrumental ensemble?

10
Are the choir/instrumental officers working to help you with visitors, guests, and prospects?

11
Are there plans to decorate the rehearsal room for the first couple of rehearsals? (It's amazing what a few colored helium balloons will do to a rehearsal room!)

12
Does the pianist, organist and/or rhythm group have the Fall music or charts so they can be working on them?

13
Does your rehearsal room say loud and clear: "Welcome!"

If you can answer yes to all those questions, you are well on the way to a successful Fall music program!

13 FIND TIME TO...

plan • dream • think • promote • minister • share yourself with someone else • prepare your music

be a better conductor • become a better musician • be a good leader of worship • work with your accompanist

get assistance where needed • read your Bible and pray • love children • kiss your wife or husband

study to show yourself approved unto God • lead your group spiritually as well as musically

14 GET OFF THE DIRECTOR'S PODIUM

Most rehearsal rooms are very nice and many have fancy director's podiums, about 4 feet square, with a very large area that has plenty of room for music, batons, breath spray, tic-tacs, towels, and Tenor Mace.

Once the director gets on that podium, he or she may tend to remain there for the whole rehearsal, without ever leaving it! I think those who do stay on the podium are missing the excitement of moving in and around and among the singers. Walking through the sections, helping the altos here or the tenors there, listening carefully to the sopranos, and working up a sweat as you conduct and work hard is important.

Remember: the group is only going to give back 80% of the energy you give to them! So if you are feeling poorly and give the choir or instrumental ensemble 80% of your energy and life, you'll get back 60%. If you give 100%, they will give back 80%. But, if you give 120%, they will give back 100% — about all you can expect from your singers. This puts the pressure on you, the conductor, to be with it, active, alive, energetic, moving around, challenging, teaching, and living the music with them. I don't think you can do that by being glued to a podium. Do you?

15 HOW TO HAVE BETTER REHEARSALS

from Tim Sharp's Sacred Music News & Reviews, *"Ideas That Will Work In Your Rehearsals"*

1

Spend a bit of time each week teaching your choir/instrumental ensemble members how to conduct an easy pattern. They may not become proficient directors, but they may grow as musicians and know more about what you're trying to communicate with your conducting gestures.

2

Memorize as often as possible! As the conductor, you should know the anthem well enough to direct if from memory! Your eye contact will lead to more eye contact from the choir to the congregation.

3

It seems the greatest trouble most often rises in the relational arena. Communicate, communicate, communicate. When you think everyone understands your plans, communicate once again

4

Never miss an opportunity to care (minister) to your flock. Hospital visits, get-well cards, anniversary/ birthday cards, knowing and acknowledging special days and events in the lives of your people will mean as much or more than any music you can teach them. The 'personal touch' is valuable.

5

Never ignore the power of a hug or handshake. Touch will make a difference, but be very careful when it involves a member of the opposite sex!

6

In rehearsal, ten minutes should not pass without you praising some element of the choir's work - a section, a person, or the whole group. Maintain a very positive attitude and never, never, never whine. The lesson here is simply: praise, praise, praise your choirs, ensembles and instrumental groups often!

7

Motivation and vision involve the senses. Make rehearsal a happenin' event using all aspects of the five senses, if possible. Make every piece of music special.

8

Give something away each week in rehearsal. This is easy to do: a left-over review or premiere cassette, a $1 McDonald's gift certificate, a package of Life Savers, a free back rub certificate, a coupon to TCBY. Be creative. Have fun with it.

9

Set an alarm or timer to go off at some point during your rehearsal. When this happens, have everyone stand, turn to the left and give their neighbor a back rub. Upon cue, everyone should sit down and go back to work. This is a great stress reliever!

10

Read a lot of music in rehearsals!

11

Embark on your own personal study of worship and begin to share it with your group. Develop a philosophy of worship and music in your church (with the appropriate leaders). Make ownership of worship broad.

12

Form a strong community base for your musical organization.

13

Bring in someone else to hear and conduct your group on a regular basis - at least twice a year. (I know, turning your choir or instrumental ensemble over to someone else can be frightening: you don't know if they can do it right, or if they do it right, the choir might enjoy them more than you!) But, bringing in someone to rehearse your group will only reinforce the things you are currently teaching them.

14

Look in a mirror and improve the person whose reflection shows up. The group *cannot* improve week by week if the director doesn't improve him or herself by study, new experiences, continuous education and new challenges. The choir or instrumental ensemble will not go where the leader is unable to lead or to go.

15

Form a strong spiritual base for your music ministry. Involve several people to assist you in this heavy responsibility.

16

Add one additional sense to your worship experience. Worship should appeal to all the senses, not just one. Every worship service should have visual, aural, and kinesthetic content. Not everyone learns or perceives the same way, so cover all bases. Also, plan worship with a team – *three heads are much better than one!*

17

Assume an operational style that functions with good organizational skills but allows in the undercurrent openness and flexibility, i.e. the workings of the Holy Spirit and a listening to God's voice. The Trinity gives us an example of bureaucratic functioning: God is the bureaucrat, Jesus is the cornerstone of human relations with one's choir members and congregation, and the Spirit is ever-present in the enabling.

18

Find someone with more expertise than you in your area of ministry, someone whom you admire and respect, and take a few private coaching sessions from that person. Spending time with someone who really knows and loves what he or she is doing in this area will likely be very rewarding; you will find yourself and your skills improving because of this personal discipline.

16 KNOW YOUR MUSIC

When the conductor's face is buried in the musical score, he or she will fail to 'connect' with the choir or congregation.

There is a worship leader in a large mega-church somewhere in the United States (the guilty shall remain nameless) who usually stands behind the pulpit and leads the congregation in worship. That's fine, but what I failed to mention is that this leader also has a notebook of music in front of him. He very often looks down at the music to see where he is. In reality, more directors do this than will admit. What's wrong with that picture?

Good question! The problem is this: when the conductor's face is buried in the musical score, he or she will fail to 'connect' with the choir or congregation and may appear to be unprepared and insincere. (An example: would it touch you if your spouse read his or her most meaningful feelings and thoughts to you from note cards?) This is something to think about if your desire is to truly lead the congregation in worship and to communicate at a peak level on a weekly basis.

So…know your music. Know it inside and out. You should know exactly what is going to happen at all times (even though surprises do occur). More importantly, you should know ahead of time your desired tempo, flow, transitions, dynamics, etc. But beyond the obvious technical aspects of the musical score, you should know how to convey the message of the song in an appropriate manner and that should be communicated to your team ahead of time.

So...know your music!

One step further. Know your music well before you rehearse the piece with anyone. The message and technical aspects should be clear in your mind if you plan on it being clear to your team members and to the congregation. There's power in knowing. So know your music!

17 MAINTAIN INTEREST IN ALL GROUPS... EVEN THOSE YOU DON'T CONDUCT

The minister of music who is learning to be a better church musician and minister cannot be interested only in the groups in which he or she is directly responsible. Other groups that do not involve him or her personally should not get less attention. This is a difficult lesson to learn. The minister of music cannot – nor should not – try to do it all! As William Easum said in his book Dancing With Dinosaurs, "Time is the new currency of the twentieth century."

The minister of music cannot, nor should not try to do it all!

Therefore, some of the work, such as graded choirs, ensembles, bell groups, or instrumental groups may end up with other directors or leaders. The growing minister of music must be as vitally interested in each of these groups as if he or she was conducting them. A good music minister multiplies him or herself over and over again to competent laypeople.

Learn to celebrate with your leadership. Encourage them, compliment them publicly, in the choir or church paper, provide opportunities for them to stretch and grow in their music leadership.

18 MAKE SURE ALL YOUR BASES ARE COVERED

When the minister of music has to be away, be it from a rehearsal or a Sunday service, it is imperative that he or she makes sure *all* rehearsals, meetings, and situations are covered. Inform your leadership that you are planning to be absent.

It never ceases to amaze that something always falls through the cracks! You can be sure that doesn't happen by making sure *all* your bases are covered, and only *you* know what those bases are!

Make sure the choir officers are prepared to take over in your absence to:

- *introduce the guess director*
- *cover the worship experience*
- *make the right announcements*
- *decide who will sing the solo, to name a few*

19 MULTI-PURPOSE REHEARSAL ROOM

Did you know that there are churches whose rehearsal room is used by a multitude of groups, from Sunday-school classes to children's choirs to other activities? There seems to be little time to get into the room before choir rehearsal to straighten the room and make it presentable for the 'next round' of people! Here's a suggestion:

Get a committee of 'choir cleaner-uppers'. Their job is to stand at the choir room door and, immediately after the other group is finished, throw open the doors and go to work straightening the chairs, picking up paper, making sure the AC is on and the room is cool, getting things out of the way and put away from the previous group, putting things in place for the choir and, at the same time, making those arriving feel welcome.

Not an easy task, but you have people in your choir who would thrive on such an assignment. I'd suggest that you change this committee every 2 to 3 months, both to give others the opportunity and to keep from wearing out the same people. Know what? You'll find the room looking cleaner as the weeks wear on because people will begin to pay more attention to keeping the room nice because of the work this committee is doing weekly.

20 NOW IS THE TIME TO BEGIN

Begin what!? Begin promotion for the Fall Music Enrollment, of course! You can't wait much longer or it will be too late. Get the information to your people ASAP so they can begin to understand the scheduling demands. Remember: people have to hear, read or see something eleven times before it sinks in. So, get to work. Here are some promotion ideas:

A
Computer-generated letters to parents, children and youth telling them about the plans for rehearsals this Fall and Christmas. Give dates.

B
A post card from your vacation telling your people how much you miss them and that you are looking forward to the new choir year. (Computer labels make this a snap!)

C
Signs and posters, along with 'Ask Me' buttons on key people each Sunday who, in the busy hallways, will tell about a particular choir or ensemble.

D
People standing up in Sunday-school classes, telling about music enrollment and plans for the Fall.

E
Personal and group visits to homes of music prospects that will surprise them!

F
August can be 'Bring a Friend to Choir or Orchestra!' Let them try it out and see if they will like it enough to stay with it in the Fall.

Now...what ideas do you have?

21 PLAN NOW FOR THE FUTURE

Oh? You're not finished with this year yet? This year is not quite over and you've got to put away the Christmas stuff? OK. Fine. I'll wait! *Dum-de-dum, dum-de-dum...*Ready? Here is a suggestion that might help with advance planning for the future:

Consider planning the service music on a three semester basis.

1. *January through May*
2. *June through August*
3. *September through December*

This is a very effective way to work through the calendar year and it matches the school calendar year. You will become aware of things to avoid on certain Sundays because of school or community activities and/or holidays. And it will provide you a working schedule for some kind of order. As a minister and a musician, you owe it to your ensemble members to keep them informed of what music is coming when. They should never walk out of Wednesday rehearsal not knowing what they are going to sing on Sunday.

Some other suggestions to work within a semester structure follow:

Never be afraid to teach new things. Remember that "Amazing Grace," "Majesty," and "Shout to the Lord" were *once* new, and had to be taught!

Vary new with the old. A good cue: if the anthem planned for a certain Sunday is new, then fill the service with lots of familiar things. If the anthem is an old, familiar, 'sugar-stick', then the service could perhaps stand a couple of newer hymns or praise choruses.

Keep 8-10 weeks of music in the folders and try to rehearse 6-9 pieces every week, in addition to major materials that are coming up. Remember: you don't have to rehearse the whole thing. Hit a section or a particular part and move on. This way, the choir members can occasionally miss a rehearsal and still be 'in the loop' with the music-learning process.

Order the music well in advance, and order ample copies so that all choir members can have their own music. They really don't like to share music!

Carefully work through each Sunday of that semester, making sure all bases are covered and every choir or group or solo that needs to be involved is scheduled.

List, on paper, the music needs, such as solos, ensembles, choir selections, children, youth, handbells, orchestra, for each service (morning and evening) for each Sunday of the semester.

Now, begin planning for the future – it's right around the corner!

22 PLAN NOW FOR CHRISTMAS

I know, it's not Easter yet, summer is toooooooo far away, and there's Fall, and choir enrollments. There's plenty of time left, you say. Not really!

Christmas plans need to be falling into place *now!* There's music to order, sets to build, costumes to design, sound and lights, script, and much, much more. Publishers will be releasing their new batch of Christmas things soon. You should be on several mailing lists to find out what's both new and good!

23 SOME OTHER CHRISTMAS IDEAS

Consider taking some of the really fine Christmas anthems and working your program around these delightful, charming and perhaps familiar pieces. Your congregation would enjoy hearing these sugar-sticks, as would the choir!

How about considering doing something that was successful a few years back — especially if your music budget is short and the music is already in the library.

Line up your orchestra *now* if you plan to hire some pros.

Consider doing *Messiah*...with orchestra! (The Christmas portion only that is.) Might be fun for your group to tackle something like this.

How about combining with your choir or instrumental group with that of a good friend and doing a program together. Once in his or her church and once in yours?

How about combining with the youth or children and making them a major part of the Christmas program? They would probably love to sing with the adults.

Remember: Christmas is just around the corner
and will be here before you can say:

"T-h-a-n-k-s-g-i-v-i-n-g!"

24 QUALITY

Everyone active in music ministry is charged by the scriptures and by our calling to quality. The word literally means the finest, the best, the choicest of the choice. God requires nothing less than the best from His servants, whether full time, part time, bi-vocational or volunteer! Quality does not necessarily mean Bach, Chopin, Handel. Quality does not necessarily mean Kirkland, Fettke, Hayes.

Quality simply means offering the best you can prepare to present to God in your worship services with the resources that are available in your music program. It is as simple as that.

> **Quality is not an alternative. It is a command from the Lord Himself.**

A word of caution: the congregation is not the audience. God is your audience. It is God to whom you are presenting your gifts of music and worship. God — and God alone. True: any music program (small church or large church) must balance the selections of music somewhat to the likes and dislikes of the congregation, but it should not tip the balance just to appease the congregation. Be very careful here.

Do the best music you can with the resources you have at your disposal. You will grow, your choir will grow, and your congregation will grow through the experience.

25 REHEARSALS SHOULD BE FUN

> *Choir and instrumental rehearsals — believe it or not — can be great therapy!*

And the rehearsal director or minister of music is the person responsible to make sure this happens! A rehearsal that is intense and filled with nothing but hard work, the chasing of notes, correcting dynamics, and a constant 'push' will soon begin to wear thin on members and directors alike! There has to be time for laughter, banter, and the lighter touch, but don't let it get out of hand. Keep a careful watch to insure that fun and laughter is in the rehearsal, but if it gets out of control you will lose the rehearsal!

Work hard, then let the group relax, read something to them gleaned from the Internet or MMEmail. Work hard, then have a testimony or sharing time. Work hard, then have someone cued to tell something funny, or serious. Work hard, then have a time of prayer. Balance your rehearsals with hard work, accomplishing what you have planned and yet, allowing the members to go home relaxed!

26 TALK LESS, WORK MORE

This may come as a surprise, but in today's fast-paced world, choir and orchestra members do not give up the comforts of home and fireplace to come to rehearsal each week just to hear what the director has to say in the rehearsal! Believe it or not, they come to work hard, learn new music, chase wrong notes, fix bad chords, have fellowship with friends, learn names of new people, and to make fun of tenors!

Try this experiment: get someone with a stopwatch (your spouse might do this for you) and ask this person to time the amount of talking you do in a rehearsal. Ask the person to total the minutes (or hours) and give it to you after rehearsal, and you'd best sit down! You will be astonished at how much of the choirs' time is spent listening to the director pontificate, and how little time is spent working on music! So...talk less and work more. Your choir will be happier, they will get better, and your spouse can put away the stopwatch!

27 TEN PRINCIPLES FOR CHOIR GROWTH *by Kennon L. Callahan*

1. Music constitutes 40% of the worship service.
2. 15% to 20% of those who attend on Sundays are potential recruits for the choir!
3. One person singing in the choir draws 1 to 3 others to church.
4. Choirs give participants a sense of family.
5. The best choirs have both quality and quantity.
6. Each service needs its own distinctive choir.
7. Because choirs are important relational groupings, they provide key ways to involve newcomers.
8. Choirs tend to grow best in multiples rather than by adding one person at a time.
9. A personal invitation to attend a rehearsal - not to join the choir - is the best way to recruit new choir members.
10. Choir growth is determined by rehearsal space, chancel space, music selection, and the choir director.

28 THREE POINTS FOR PERFECTION

1

Listen, listen, listen…to good music, created by the best people, no matter what genre. It is amazing what this can do for your musical growth, and listening to good music of all genres will expand your range and repertoire.

2

Make sure rehearsals are fun! This means, simply, enjoyable for those who come to choir or instrumental ensemble. With today's schedules, time frames, and windows of opportunity, rehearsal should be something worth the valuable time of your people. Every week's rehearsal should include: learning, singing, laughing, fellowship, refreshments, prayer, and always something new!

3

Keep your rehearsal room neat, clean, chairs straight, fresh smelling, with waste baskets empty. Have extra music available and close by. Change your room around often, keeping posters, bulletin boards, hangings, and message boards up-to-date.

29 TOP FIVE SECRETS TO BEING HAPPY

Have you ever noticed people's reactions when a highway is closed because of an accident or some other unusual event? Some listen to the radio, a few might begin tossing a Frisbee, others might seem to be working or reading, while still others might opt for a quick nap. In spite of the other handful who are clearly agitated and angry, pacing about, swearing and upset, most have decided that the best response to this event, which none of us could control, is to be happy.

Remember Bobby McFerrin's hit song, "Don't Worry, Be Happy"?

Five tips to increase happiness in your life:

Decide to be a happy person

Abraham Lincoln said: "Most people are about as happy as they make up their minds to be." As he observed, most people, most of the time, can choose how stressed, happy, troubled, or relaxed they wish to be. Choose to be happy.

Watch TV news less

We don't need the stress that both local and national TV can bring. It's all about the very worst of humanity. So…just don't watch.

Take time

Dogs can teach us a lot of things: loyalty, noticing the sights, sounds, and smells in the yard, and being relaxed and playing. They also teach us to eat when we are hungry, to nap when you need it, and to get our ears scratched whenever possible!

Laugh everyday

Hear a joke. Tell a joke. Learn to laugh at one's self. Laugh with your friends and family and co-workers. There are very few medicines as powerful as laughter, and you can't overdose, although it is addicting!

Practice the 'attitude of gratitude'

We all have much for which to be grateful. Just try thanking the many people who assist us, encourage us, teach us and open doors for us and you'll discover this could take all day!

30 TWENTY-FIVE WAYS TO BEGIN A NEW YEAR

1 Give more than your people expect...and do it cheerfully.

2 Memorize your music.

3 When you say, "I love you," mean it.

4 When you say, "I'm sorry," look the person in the eye.

5 Be engaged at least six months before you get married.

6 Believe in love at first sight.

7 Never laugh at anyone's dreams.

8 Love deeply/passionately. You might get hurt, but it's the only way to live!

9 Don't judge people by their relatives.

10 Talk slowly but think quickly.

11 Remember that great love and great achievements involve great risk.

12 Call your Mom, often.

13 Remember the three R's:

• Respect for self • Respect for others • Responsibility for all your actions

14 Don't let a little dispute injure a great friendship.

15 When you realize you've made a mistake, take steps to correct it.

16 Smile when picking up the phone. The caller will hear it in your voice.

17 Spend some quality time alone.

18 Open your arms to change, but don't let go of your values.

19 Remember that silence is sometimes the best answer.

20 Read more books and watch less TV. Read one book a month - minimum!

21 Live a good, honorable life. Then when you get older and think back, you'll get to enjoy it a second time.

22 Trust in God, but lock your car.

23 Spend time alone, with God. What you learn will overflow into your music.

24 Stretch your personal skills.

25 Get outside your own little world and experience a fuller life.

31 YOU CAN'T DO IT ALL YOURSELF

One of the major battles the minister of music has to fight all the time is time! Out of this great respect for time might come the desire to do far more than is expected! The wise minister of music should not even attempt to do every rehearsal, every performance, every solo, direct every choir, or do everything by him or herself. I know of a minister of music who personally directs or is responsible for 16 groups, and my friends, that is far too many.

Get help!

Part of the responsibility of being a faithful minister of music is building good and effective leadership. If the music ministry comes to a dead stop when a minister of music resigns and moves on, then this music minister has failed the church! When he or she departs the scene, the program should be able to continue for a while because of the leadership he or she has put into place during the ministry. Train leaders. Train helpers. Train! Train! Train! Provide encouragement and funds to keep the leadership up-to-date. You can't do it all yourself, so don't even try.

32 VISION AND PASSION

One of the watchwords of today's church is – or should be – vision. To have vision is to have the ability to be able to see what is not yet here. If our vision comes from God, then we must also have a passion for it. Passion fuels vision! If you don't have an emotional fire and heartfelt enthusiasm known as passion, you won't have true vision. But, there are passion destroyers that can keep us from having the passion that God wants us to stir in the hearts of our people — and even within our own hearts. These passion destroyers include:

Selfish greed
everything that is done is done for 'me', and not for the kingdom

Physical fatigue
from overworking, overeating, over-stressing and not overcoming

Ego trips
one of the great stumbling blocks to a great ministry

Distraction
anything that gets in the way of our passion and vision

Bitterness
a bitter heart and spirit quenches the Spirit

Unwillingness to change
afraid to take a new step or offer a new challenge for fear of rejection

Lack of focus
if we can't focus, how do we expect our people to focus!

Disobedience
to the will of God for our lives

33 VOCAL WARM-UPS

Because most church-choir conductors have such a short amount of rehearsal time each week, the time given to vocal warm-ups is often tossed aside and we just 'jump in' and begin singing – as if the choir members have vocalized and gotten their voices prepared and ready on their own. Not!

Talk little, sing lots!

What to do? A good, workable solution is to begin rehearsal with a familiar selection that the choir knows well, that is in a low register, and, even better, has a good unison section! A familiar chorus will also work. Listen carefully to tune the unison sound. Don't sing with the choir! Just listen. Go to a section that has part work and again, *listen* to the sections to make sure the overall sound is balanced, natural, and blended.

Encourage their singing, and compliment often. You will get more out of the choir by loving on them than by chiding them with dark humor. After this brief time, five minutes max, the choir will be ready to sing for you with a much better, more relaxed spirit and voice!

Fellowship and Ministry

34 A GOOD TIME TO MINISTER

You might be surprised to learn that some of the most effective ministry you can do with your choir or instrumental members can be done prior to rehearsal on Wednesday night! If you can't have rehearsal till after Prayer Meeting, try to make yourself available to be among the people twenty minutes or so ahead of the downbeat of rehearsal. You will find yourself overwhelmed by the amount of information you can gather from your members.

A good thing to do is to have the Social Committee provide *weekly* coffee, juice, and cookies or chips for those early birds to munch on. This will be a good break for them and it will provide a much needed energy boost before they come under your direction. It will be a good break for you, too.

You will discover needs, prayer requests, tidbits about the family unit, cares, things for which to be grateful and you can offer private prayer, scripture, advice, and counsel, all within the confines of the choir room, and on an individual level. This also gives the choir members opportunity to be with you, away from the director's stand, one-on-one, so to speak. It puts them on your level, or better yet, it puts you on their level for a brief time. You will find that this time will become very important to you, and to them. So…get out of the office, get away from the computer, get away from Prayer Meeting after you lead the hymn/chorus and get into the rehearsal room area among your people! It will pay great dividends. It works!

35 AN ENCOURAGER

As you enlist workers, helpers, and others to participate in the music ministry – from children's choir leaders, handbell leaders, orchestra leaders, secretaries, even the helpers in Youth Choir – do you encourage and appreciate them often?

It is often easy to enlist people to serve and then get busy and forget about them, because the assignment is running smoothly, there are no problems, and things are fine.

Remember: As a music minister, the less you are involved in a group, the less likely you are to pay close attention to it! In other words: if you don't direct it, you tend to forget about it! Make sure you compliment your leadership often. Send personal or computer-generated thank-you notes often. Pop in on a rehearsal, just to say "Hello!" Watch the reaction of both the participants and the leadership! They will be surprised that you would come to visit their rehearsal and to affirm their work! You can *never* say thank you enough! And when people do nice things for you, say nice things about you, or give you something special, be sure to write a personal thank-you note! That is a sure sign of appreciation, and we are living in a time when real 'appreciation' is becoming a bygone product! Don't you contribute to its death!

Be an Encourager!

36

AN OLD GERMAN PROVERB

We are too soon old, and too late smart.

Wow, what a great thought!

In my early ministry, I often wondered how long it would take for me to get respect. I wondered when deacons, pastors, other staff, choir members, and church members would begin to recognize that I did have something to say and that I wanted and needed to say it. Perhaps, that was the problem! Maybe they were not ready to hear what I had to say at that time in my ministry, and maybe I wasn't *really* ready to have a platform to say anything at that time!

I began to think of all the people of whom I had a great amount of respect, and why I respected them, and I discovered that most of those dear people were older, more mature, and wise, perhaps beyond their years. One such person was my dear, late friend Jim Woodward. He taught me so much and loved me in those early years of discovering who I was and what I had to contribute to the world of church music — he listened to me and gave me opportunity to minister! Gene Bartlett was another friend who always provided college and seminary students opportunities to serve. He was indeed wise.

I discovered that the older one becomes, the more people tend to want to listen, to ask for advice, to desire counsel. And this is the way it should be, for with maturity comes wisdom, with experience comes know-how, and with longevity in ministry comes a stableness that leads to security.

Patience is a great teacher.

37 APPRECIATION

One of the golden keys to effective leadership is showing appreciation of other people. One just can't appreciate people too much! As leaders, we sometimes get so busy that we forget to drop a thank-you note to those who participated in worship last week or fixed the refreshments for choir or instrumental fellowship. Everyone who works with any part of the upcoming Christmas experience should receive a thank-you letter or note from the minister of music soon after the event. This includes the graded-choir staff, instrumentalists, accompanists, directors of other choirs, ensembles, drama people, set designers, costume people and others. With today's modern technology, this can be done on computer and personally signed without too much hassle, and it will be worth it in the long run!

> **Appreciation: A Golden Key to Leadership**

You can't appreciate people too much and it takes just a little time.

38 BALANCE OR BURNOUT

Life can be overwhelming, can't it? The demands on our time, energy, emotions and skills hit us from all sides, all while the pendulum of life still swings. Balance is needed if we are to retain our effectiveness and cutting-edge in ministry, and avoid burnout. In the process, our family, ministry and our perspective on life will suffer or become distorted, and our walk with Jesus will become habit or routine.

How can one know if his or her life is out of balance?

You begin to feel inadequate

...or alone, worthless and/or fearful. Self-esteem is affected when your life is out-of-balance. You stop looking at things through the eyes of Jesus and begin to use your own eyes, or worse yet, the eyes of others! A recent survey says that 70% of religious leaders have a lower self-image now than when they first entered the ministry! Remember: how you see yourself affects how you relate to family, friends, subordinates and colleagues.

You have difficulty sensing God

You cease to hear God's voice in your life and activity. There is no closeness that once characterized your relationship to God. If you are having trouble hearing God speak, you're in trouble at the very heart of Christian leadership!

You lack joy and fulfillment

Habit, duty and obligation now are the result of the things that once brought you joy and fulfillment. Doing things by rote is much less enjoyable than by choice.

MORE

Realize that nothing of value is accomplished apart from the leadership of God in our lives. Realize that health, family and ministry are more important than programs or schedules! If we could only learn this fact of life!! Cut back today to build a balance for tomorrow. If you don't, there may not be a tomorrow!

39 BEGIN *NOW* TO PLAN YOUR FAMILY VACATION

So many times, the family vacation will sneak up on us, and we will (1) plan too late to get any good deals, just ignore it and continue working (a very bad idea), or (2) go anyway and be frustrated because you didn't get the plans in the works sooner!

So…now is the time. Have a 'family council' and discuss the vacation: how long, where the family would like to go, and other details. Put someone in charge of beginning the process of developing plans. Phone calls can be made, emails can be sent, and the best prices and places to stay can be obtained, then brought back to the family council for final approval. Some responsibility might even be assigned to older children! This allows them to feel as if they have had an important part in the event. Make all the plans early, cover every detail, and, before you know it, the time will be here and a grand time will be had by all.

Every staff member in the Vineyard *should* take their full and allotted vacation whether or not the pastor takes his or hers! It is very important for you to be with your family for an extended time rather than give all your time, energy, and self to the ministry. You deserve a break today!

40 BEYOND THE WALLS OF THE CHURCH

> *In every opportunity to perform, there is an opportunity for ministry.*

The Christmas season is just around the corner! And with it, one of the best times of the year for your groups to go beyond the 'walls of the church' and spread the seeds of the Gospel throughout the community. In every opportunity to perform, there is an opportunity for ministry.

Here are a few suggestions:

Seasonal Community Events

Most cities have holiday events and ask for groups to perform: an airport concert, a concert welcoming visitors to your city, the annual community Christmas tree lighting, outdoor concerts and/or holiday meals for the homeless. The Chamber of Commerce can assist in finding out about such events and how you can participate!

Ongoing Opportunities

The same groups requested for community events can be used for everyday opportunities, like nursing homes, prisons, or shopping malls. These people are always so appreciative! You will be blessed far more than you could imagine! Nursing homes and prisons are easy to contact. Just call them! Very few will turn down an opportunity to have a volunteer group come to spread a little 'hope' through music. Many will allow you to openly share the Gospel. Shopping malls are open to groups, but are hesitant to have you share your faith either verbally or musically. Still, it is an opportunity for exposure of your church to the community. You can call the mall office or property management company, whose offices are normally located in the business offices on site.

Get outside the walls of the 'fortress' and share your music ministry with your city!

41 CARDS ARE APPRECIATED

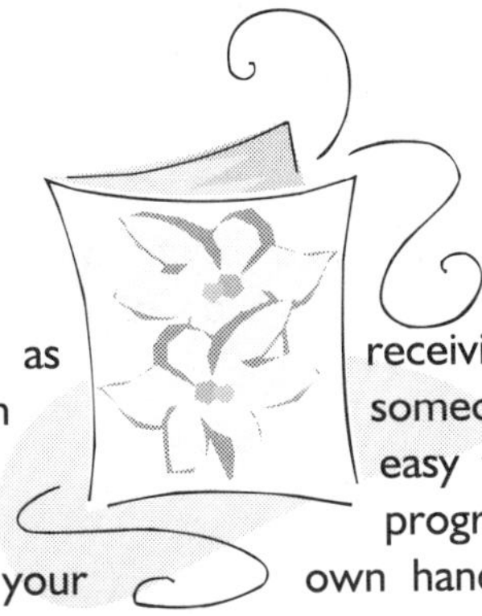

Nothing pleases one as much as receiving a birthday, anniversary or special occasion card from someone who cares. With today's modern technology, this is an easy task, even with large mailing lists! There is even a handwriting program available for both MAC and IBM machines that can translate your own handwriting into a font on your computer!

Computer-generated labels are also a big help. Group by month all of the birthdays, anniversaries, and other dates of celebration for each member of the group you wish to send cards to (your adult choir, for example) and let your computer generate labels. Then, toward the end of a given month, prepare cards or notes for those occasions in the following month. After signing the card, put them in an envelope, already addressed thanks to the labels, and they are ready to mail! For those occasions that fall between the 1st and 15th of the month, send the cards on the 30th of the previous month. For those occasions that occur in the later half of the month, send cards around the 12th of that same month. It works! People appreciate your thoughtfulness.

This idea also works well if you go on a vacation or extended trips. You can take a set of labels and send post cards back from your vacation site to let your people know you are thinking of them while you are away, and you are because you are sending them a postcard! Good PR is in reach of most of us!

42 CHOIR GIVE-AWAYS

Everyone enjoys an unexpected gift! Ever so often, treat your choir to a surprise or three! Tape a surprise under several chairs; mid-way through rehearsal, in the 'stand and stretch time', tell the choir to check under their chairs for a surprise! Use candy bars, CDs, cassettes, TCBY certificates, or a host of other surprises. The choir member who receives one will be thrilled! It is a fun way to relax, enjoy the moment, and get rid of the ton of CDs and/or cassettes that come across your desk regularly that you probably won't use!

43 CHRISTMAS CARDS

Yes, they are expensive.
Yes, they take a lot of time.
Yes, they can be a pain and a bother.
Yes, it isn't something that a busy minister of music likes to do.

But, if you will purchase (or make) a Christmas card for everyone involved in your music ministry — from choir/instrumental ensemble members to directors — and mail it to them around the second week of December, your people will be so touched and affected by your thought of them that they will tend to be just a little bit more faithful, because you cared enough to send them a greeting!

And, as you get involved in it, you will discover an enjoyment in writing each person this personal note as you remember what it is about him or her that you enjoy! Try it! You'll want to do it again, perhaps at Easter.

44 CLIMATE CONTROL

Ever notice that every home has its own unique fragrance or climate, sometimes called ambiance. Perhaps you can recall the particular aroma of the home in which you grew up or remember the smell in the home of your grandparents. Application of this concept can also be made to the church where you serve as a leader. There is a climate, a fragrance, an ambiance that your team members get when they are with you and under your leadership. They may not be able to verbalize it – but the fragrance is there and they just know it.

That fragrance, climate, or ambiance may be described in different ways:

cheerful / sad

healthy / unhealthy

stretch and grow / don't rock the boat

dream the dream / sleep on it

upbeat / downbeat

go for it / hold back

encouraging / discouraging

challenge the status quo / status quo is okay

optimistic / pessimistic

Whether you say it or not, the ambiance is there. In a healthy climate, there will be positive, high-energy level performance. Relationships will be authentic and vibrant. People will feel fulfilled in what they do. They will enjoy being in the environment where you are as their leader.

How would you diagnose the ambiance in your music ministry at this moment?

A leader's primary role is 'climate control'. The passive leader who simply permits a 'whatever' climate to develop will see mediocrity and often a lack of purpose among his or her fellowship. Climate control takes intentionality.

A leader's primary role is 'climate control.'

Leaders must be lifelong learners in staff/team leadership development. The Bible, of course, is our primary source, but like Jesus, we can draw from everyday life by:

A	B	C	D	E
Attending training opportunities available to you.	Continually reading books on leadership. Always be reading!	Networking with other leaders via email, phone or personal conferences.	Getting out of our own private fortress. If we don't, we may watch the world pass by, thinking we are on the cutting edge of life when, in reality, our cutting edge might be rather dull.	Staying fresh and up-to-date on articles related to your areas of expertise by using such resources as *Creator* magazine, *The Choral Journal* (the magazine of the American Choral Directors' Association), and *USA Today.*

If you are a leader, make sure you are creating a good climate or ambiance for those who follow you. It will pay great dividends in the future.

45 COMMISSION MUSICIANS TO MISSION MINISTRY

Mission or smaller churches in your area are hampered by the lack of musicians in their membership. Consider commissioning one or two members of your music ministry to go as a 3-6 month music missionaries to help with congregational singing, children's choirs, accompanying, or worship planning. Most larger churches have a wealth of musicians — some of whom are doing almost nothing in ministry. This is a great way to awaken the Spirit of Christ in them, and involve them in missions! Plan a formal commissioning in an evening service. Give a plaque or certificate and send them on their way. Check on them often and see how you or the church can minister as they minister. All will find great spiritual and musical rewards.

46 COMMISSIONING OF MUSICIANS

Here is a suggested commissioning service for someone who has responded to the Call of God into full-time music ministry:

Pastor (or Minister of Music): Dear Friends, it is always a pleasure and a privilege for this church to recognize those who have responded to the Call of God into the ministry of music. To conduct, to sing, the skills of organization and the ability to play instruments are all ministries of Christ to those He has called into His Vineyard of Service. The support and the prayers of this congregation are vital to any ministry. Making music — to the praise of God — and the ability to lead musical ensembles and the congregation in such praise is a ministry that requires devotion and discipline.

(Name) stands before us today, answering God's call on his/her (say just one) life into music ministry. This acceptance of God's call has come through much prayer, dialogue and realization that indeed, God has definitely called him/her (say just one) into music ministry. Do you (first name), accept responsibility for this ministry?

Reply: I do.

Pastor: Will you be faithful to the disciplines required of music and will you follow God's leadership in your life as you continue in this ministry?

Reply: I will.

Pastor: May the faith expressed by your music live in your heart, and what you believe in your heart, may you practice in your life. May God give you grace to offer your music and your life in faithfulness and consecration to God's people. Would you like the opportunity to tell your friends about your call to music ministry?

Reply: I would like to do this. (Person then gives his or her personal testimony about God's call upon his or her life)

Pastor: Dear Friends, I commend to you (first name). To him/her (say just one) has been given the opportunity to be a part of and to study for the ministry of music in the church. Will you sustain him/her (say just one) with your encouragement and your prayers, as together we seek to offer praise to God?

Congregation: We will.

Pastor: Now (first name) will kneel at the front of the church, and I extend to anyone who wishes to do so to come and lay hands on him/her (circle one) and give a scripture promise or a prayer for music ministry. You may now come.

Closing Prayer (Pastor): O Lord, I pray You would bless (first name) as he/she (say just one) begins the disciplines of music ministry. I pray You would guide him/her in the paths You would have them travel. May Your imprint be upon his or her music ministry. May he or she be a strong spiritual leader as well as deeply committed to music. I pray for fullness of heart as You lead and guide him/her (say just one) to fulfill this commitment. May we, as a church family, be constant in prayer, holding him/her (say just one) up to Your throne in season and out of season. Bless us this day. In the strong Name of Jesus Christ, I pray. Amen.

47 FINDING WAYS TO COPE IN GOD'S CREATED WORLD

Balance your life

Life is not meant to be all of everything, but a balance of many elements. At the end of the month, do a quick check to see if one area of your life is out - of - balance; if something is off, correct it.

Relax

Don't take yourself too seriously. Practice being calm. Take a break. Take sufficient time away. Engage in some leisure activity. Take a deep breath. Read scripture (Psalms/ Proverbs are excellent).

Laugh and play

Laughter promotes endorphins. A sense of humor is a gift. Smile. Take time very day to recreate and do something you enjoy. Pursue a hobby. Learn to play, and play. Take care of your "childlike nature."

Monitor the pace of your life

Exercise reasonable control over the access that people have to you. Limit that access so as to pace your stressors. Remember: the better you are at what you do, the more people will want from you. You must be willing to say no!

Create buffer zones

Develop and consistently practice habits and rituals that are stable and secure. Create small buffer zones between some of your obligations. Even 10 minutes allows you time to catch up, close your eyes, pray, call your spouse, and defuse your own tension.

Be spontaneous

Plan for free time. Christ's lifestyle was responsive to the present and often spontaneous. Isn't that a signal to us?

Get enough sleep

Relax before going to bed. Wake up and go to bed about the same time everyday. If you wake up worrying, jot down the worry and tell yourself to think about it in the morning.

Get outdors.

This helps regain perspective.

48 FINDING WAYS TO COPE...WITH GOD

CLARIFY YOUR VALUES Know and live in peace with what you believe and cherish. Live out these convictions.

TREASURE GOD'S WORD Memorize Scripture. Read uplifting books. Listen to great music.

SET REALISTIC GOALS Write down your goals. Plan intelligently. Know what you wish to accomplish, then set small, easily attainable objectives. Visualize yourself reaching these goals and reward yourself for completing each step.

PRUNE COMMITMENTS It is more difficult to stop something than to start it! Get the clippers and prune away activities that are no longer necessary. Turn off the TV, and the computer!

PRACTICE SIMPLICITY

Be content with less. Recognize that unnecessary possessions are 'stealers of divine time' as we maintain 'things'. Spend more time on opportunities that have eternal significance, like your family. Learn to serve, to love, and to spend less on things that soon leave you forever.

MANAGE YOUR TIME

Set up a calendar, block out some project time, and provide free time. Be realistic, and allow enough time, early on, for projects. Avoid last minute rushes. Learn to delegate! Plan time to 'create'.

49 FINDING WAYS TO COPE...WITH OTHERS

USE YOUR ENERGY EFFECTIVELY

Deal with your greatest stressor when you have your greatest energy.

ANTICIPATE STRESS

Think ahead about possible stressful events and plan ways to respond. Expect the unexpected.

DEVELOP YOUR PROBLEM-SOLVING SKILLS

Identify the problem and write it down so it is clear in your mind

Brainstorm and list all ideas that might help

Clarify your options; list the pros and cons

Choose a 'best' solution; just having a plan reduces stress

Plan what you will do, when, and with whom

Put your plan into action

Evaluate your plan: what worked, what didn't work

REDUCE JOB STRESS

Work smart, prioritize correctly, maintain a schedule, take short breaks. Don't let trivial things get you. Celebrate if you are doing well. Set one goal that will assist with your work load.

DEVELOP A NEW SKILL

Do not count on past training and skills to last forever! Keep current of new knowledge in your field and learn new ways to do things. How long has it been since you attended a conference outside your church?

CHOOSE TO FORGIVE OTHERS, AS WELL AS YOURSELF

Forgiveness will go a long way in reducing your stress levels.

SPEND TIME WITH PEOPLE WHO ARE GOOD FOR YOU

Find that special person – friend, relative, colleague, counselor, pastor – and build a relationship with one who cherishes and appreciates you and who is not trying to change you. It takes time to develop and keep trusted relationships. Talking to others relieves stress and puts troubles in proper perspective.

50 FINDING WAYS TO COPE...WITH YOURSELF

Avoid caffeine and tranquilizers

Relieving pressure temporarily with these actually intensifies stress.

Avoid wrongdoing and sin

"Turn from evil" (Proverbs 4:27)

Write

One study has shown that people who write about traumatic events had stronger immune systems within 4 days. Keep a journal. Write about the situation every time you feel stressed — with whom you are with, where you are, and how you feel.

Pursue positive life choices

Time for yourself, to read, listen to music, think, and to spend with family and friends to share the richness of life.

Exercise

Physical activity works out stress. Walking is one of the best forms of exercise, giving a sense of well being and helping to control pain. Walk with your spouse and each of you can share the high and low points of your day!

Eat well

Eat balanced meals. In a sense, we are what we eat. Fruits and veggies are best. Limit salt. Drink lots of water.

Choose to have a good attitude

Learn to look for the kind, the positive, the loving things in people and situations. Focus on the good and the beautiful. (Philippians 4:8)

Believe in yourself

Believe in the person that God has designed you to be. Do your best, but don't expect personal perfection. Focus on the positive, recall past successes. Don't take things personally when they go wrong. Know your strengths. Play to those strengths. Associate with positive people. Write out 'positive affirmations' to remind yourself of your best qualities. Count your blessings!

51 FIRST THINGS FIRST

Leaders prioritize their time, perhaps not even realizing that in their choice of time, they are doing exactly what they want to do, because it is tied to their personal purpose.

What leaders think is important is where they are going to spend the majority of their time!

Every person on the earth has 168 hours per week. Regardless of wealth or station in life, no one has less and none have more.

Leaders are stressed at every level by people continually asking for their time, and most leaders have a very difficult time in saying no. Leaders fear that if they say "No," they won't be asked again, or they will hurt someone's feelings, or the opportunity just seems to be too good to turn down, or they think one more thing in an already crowded schedule won't hurt, or they think someone else won't do it like they can do it.

Leaders should be prepared to notice negative and subtle changes in family or job that are brought on by too much outside responsibility. Some of these changes might include:

Irritability

Sharp words

Anger

Loneliness

Ignoring

Frustration

Fear

A leader should list the important things in his or her life and adhere to that list religiously! High priorities for good leaders should be:

Quality time *in personal devotions* – It's hard to lead without instructions from the Boss.

in renewal and updating of the leader's best disciplines – A leader can't give and give without some renewal and inspiration from an outside source.

with spouse – Away from kids; walks, and reflective and romantic time.

with children – Ice cream after school, special Saturday breakfast.

with grandchildren – Letters, cards, phone calls, surprises.

spent on the position or job – make sure your best shot is involved in your job and you aren't giving the best away somewhere else.

Recreation An absolute must for leader survival.

Learn to say "No" more often – It gets easier with practice.

Things a leader might consider pruning:

Assignments that are low items on the personal scale	Activities that take the leader away regularly from family and job	Activities that are similar in nature that can be cut without much concern	Time spent on things not important to family, job or calling

Just because your boss is a workaholic, that is no reason for you to follow in his or her footsteps and be on the course for an early heart attack, family problems, nervous breakdown, job stress, and more!

Time is a priority. Use it wisely!

52 FIVE HUNDRED ANTHEMS? IN ONE LIBRARY? COME ON!

Do you know how long it would take to sing 500 anthems, one per Sunday and not repeat any anthem? 9.6 years! Someone bragged to me once that he had 2,600 anthems in the music library! My question to him was: what do you intend to do with 2,600 anthems? How many years would it take to sing every one of those anthems, without repeating any? Answer: 50 years!

So, **why not consider setting a limit on the number of anthems your library will hold and stop there.** If you have reached that number, the next time you purchase a new anthem, cull out one in the library that is out-of-date, has too few copies, is dog-eared or out-of-style, or any number of other reasons, and give it away to a smaller church or mission! This is good stewardship – it will give you additional library space, allow you to help a struggling church, and you will be keeping your library up-to-date.

53 GRATITUDE IS A FORM OF WISDOM

It's Christmas, or Easter, or Summer. People are harried, frazzled, anxious, uptight, overly busy, stressed and even sometimes angry. A heart of honest gratitude can relieve much of the tension in most people. I would encourage you to write notes of gratitude and expressions of thanks to all who have participated or are participating in your Christmas music production(s). They will be pleased you remembered them in this thoughtful manner. A simple, handwritten note of gratitude will usually be kept, to be read over and over again when things get tough.

Remember: **You can never appreciate people enough!** Lavish them with compliments, gratitude and thanks. They will return to work with you again and again when you honor them with gratitude. The scriptures teach this. People love to receive words of compliment. It is so easy to do, yet so hard sometimes to accomplish. Do it soon before it is too late, and the season is past!

54 GROWING PIANISTS IN YOUR CHURCH

One of the best ways to develop more church accompanists is to have the less experienced instrumentalists play along with the regular accompanists during the congregational singing. There is less pressure on them, and these young people can begin to feel comfortable starting to play in services more quickly if they realize that they are not the only accompanist. During the Sunday-evening service, bring in an extra keyboard and let these maturing accompanists play along with the regular pianist/organist. Perhaps only playing the melody right now, with the volume is so low that no one in the congregation can hear, but God can and they will gain valuable experience!

If we don't do something soon,
we will have no pianists or organists — period!

55 GUEST ARTISTS

So, you've decided to bring in an outside artist to sing in your service(s). Great! But let me ask a question. Why are you bringing them in? A bad choice of an outside artist can destroy what you are trying to build in your church.

There are artists out there that

are more interested in money than in ministry. You read it first here!!

will not perform in churches anymore, just in large venues.

will put on a good show, but fail to really minister or lead the congregation to worship.

On the other hand, guest artists can be wonderful additions to existing ministries within the church. They can bring encouragement, inspiration, and exhortation to the church and to your music ministry. Music people can be challenged to 'raise the bar' in their abilities, their commitment, and their relationship with the Lord.

How can artists be utilized intentionally?

Only bring in artists that match your church's worship style.

Have the artist(s) sing some with your choir or praise team. For instance, they could sing the solo on a choral piece.

If their schedule permits, bring them in on a Sunday morning and have them sing 2-3 songs as appropriate in *your* carefully planned service. I would even go so far as to ask for specific songs from the artist that will match what you're planning in your service. Then have the artist do a full concert that evening. This gives your people an extended time with the artist to build a relationship.

Bring in an artist for special occasions such as Easter, July 4th, early Christmas, conferences, women/men's retreats, etc.

The bottom line is that you should include the bringing-in of outside artists into your budget or know that you can raise the necessary funds through love offerings or ticket sales. You should be able to clearly articulate your reasons for bringing them in. The pros must definitely outweigh the cons. Appropriately planned guest artist appearances can add a spark to your services and fire up the music ministry and congregation. This is an idea that will work in any size church. You just may have to come up with a creative way to fund it.

56 HONOR YOUR ACCOMPANISTS

If you are fortunate enough to have good accompanists, good musicians, supporters of the music ministry, able to leap tall buildings with a single *glissando,* then you are most fortunate, indeed. You should, of course, go to bat for them in budget time for a nice increase in salary. You should recognize their birthday or anniversary as pianist/organist for the church. And once in a while, celebrate them for no reason by having an after choir party honoring the accompanists! It will pay great dividends down the road.

57 HOLY THINGS

BE CAREFUL
BE AWARE
BE SENSITIVE
BE CONCERNED

Be always on the alert that you treat 'holy things' with the right kind of respect. It is very easy for those in ministry, who are around holy things everyday, to become somewhat callous regarding the things your people regard as holy. This becomes that much more of an issue for those of us who are in the church building almost every day, especially during the Christmas season.

I remember how shocked I was when I was visiting a minister of music. As we walked through the beautiful sanctuary, he was showing me the set for the Christmas program. Someone had left a gold cross out of place, and so he picked up and carelessly tossed it over in a corner. I dare say that if a member of the church had seen that act, there would have been some apology forthcoming and soon. Our people respect and love their sanctuary buildings and all the elements therein, as should we. Be always careful to respect holy things.

58 HOW LONG HAS IT BEEN SINCE YOU…

Complimented someone, and really meant it?

Sent someone a note of appreciation for a job well-done?

Encouraged someone by phone or personal visit?

Spent time with a colleague and helped him better himself?

Attended a music conference that refreshed your soul and musical skills?

Prayed for your pastor?

Challenged your choir(s) to be better than they think they are?

Were 'right on', prepared, and knowledgeable in a choir rehearsal, and your people knew and responded to it?

Isn't it about time you did some of these things?

59 HOW LONG HAS IT BEEN SINCE YOU…

…left the safety and security of your church office and attended a real music conference, with classes that would improve your conducting skills, keyboard skills, and vocal skills? Watched someone who had good rehearsal techniques, or took any steps to improve your own personal musical skills?

In today's world, with its fast-paced society, everyone in ministry has to stay abreast of the times, such as new music, technology, techniques, concepts, and ideas.

You heard it here first: if we don't stay up-to-date then staleness will begin to set in. We can't keep performing the same pieces – those 'war horses' that are our most favorites – year after year. We can't continue to conduct the same way time after time. Multi-rhythm is a mainstay these days. We can't continue to administrate the exact same way we did in 1967 or 1977! I urge you to find a good music workshop or music conference this Spring or Summer and get yourself involved in finding out what is new or what you can learn that is fresh. You will learn something new…guaranteed! Plus, we will have many wonderful surprises, meaningful worship, and fellowship. Just do it!

I am constantly amazed at the numbers of men and women who graduate from college and/or seminary and never again go anywhere to learn anything new, exciting, challenging or meaningful to their ministry.

60 HOW TO AVOID BURNOUT

Short-term Goals

KNOW YOURSELF
Play to your strengths.

WORK SMART
Rather than working hard, learn to delegate.

SET REALISTIC GOALS
Plan for what you can do.

TAKE A BREAK IN A DIFFERENT WAY
Do something memorable or even wild.

CHANGE YOUR ROUTINE
Do something new. Alter harmful routines.

DON'T TAKE THINGS PERSONALLY
Ever.

CHOOSE TO FORGIVE OTHERS
Even when they don't deserve it.

BUILD A RESOURCE NETWORK
Develop a new friend.

DEVELOP AN OUTSIDE HOBBY
Or outside interest.

SCHEDULE THE COMING WEEK CORRECTLY
Build in time to relax and think and create.

Long-term Strategies

RE-PRIORITIZE YOUR LIFE

DISTINGUISH URGENT FROM IMPORTANT
Make time for the important (family!).

TAKE PROPER CONTROL OF YOUR LIFE
Be responsible.

GET PROPER REST AND RELAXATION
Eat right and exercise.

DEVELOP LONG-TERM GOALS
You don't have to do it all right now.

CONSIDER CHANGING JOBS
Talk to someone you trust about this.

GET INTO A CHRISTIAN SUPPORT GROUP
...which includes Christian counseling, if necessary.

61 HOW TO CREATE STAFF 'TEAMSMANSHIP'

A
Send notes of encouragement and appreciation.

B
Share clippings, email materials, book reviews.

C
Compliment from the pulpit or in the church paper or in church activities.

D
Have lunch on regular basis with casual conversation.

E
Play racquetball or basketball games, golf, tennis, or go fishing.

F
Be positive of fellow staffers when in public.

62 HOW TO GUARD YOUR TIME WITH SPOUSE AND CHILDREN

1 Learn to say the magic word: NO!

2 Go on a date with your spouse at least twice a month.

3 Leave work early often to play with your kids, while they are still kids.

4 Take one full day off per week for family, not hobbies.

63 HOW TO KEEP YOUR CHOIRS/ENSEMBLES MOTIVATED

1
Keep rehearsals moving and versatile.

2
Share Max Lucado thoughts or other things you are reading in devotional times.

3
Plan fun give-aways and trivia questions.

4
Allow for prayer and praise time in rehearsal, including the hymns/choruses for next week's worship service.

MORE

5	6	7	8
Always try to sing something from memory, at least some of the time.	Move choir rehearsal to another night.	Have a fast-paced and exciting rehearsal plan.	Laugh a lot.

64 HOW TO KEEP YOUR CHURCH OUT OF TROUBLE

A CHURCH OR SCHOOL DOES NOT HAVE THE RIGHT TO

COPY ANY MUSIC

OF ANY KIND

FOR ANY REASON

WITHOUT PERMISSION

FROM THE PUBLISHER

Many ministers of music think that because the church has purchased a CCLI license, they can legally copy music. This not true. A CCLI license does not give you the right to copy anthems or orchestra scores or handbell scores or keyboard scores or video frames!

Look for the best discount possible and purchase the music, but don't photocopy anything without permission! It could get the church into serious legal and financial trouble. Just don't do it!

65 JUST SAY NO!

Why don't you take a moment at the beginning of this new week, look at your personal and church calendar to see how many things to which you could have said "No." Then, after you have determined the 3, 4, or 12 things that you have accepted but should not have, work at trying to make contact with the persons involved to see if a "No" would be proper!

Remember: *you* are the keeper of your personal calendar, and no date gets on that calendar unless you put it there! With the approaching busy and stressful holiday season, it is going to become more and more important not to calendar some things so you can spend some time with spouse and children.

66 LET THE CONGREGATION HEAR SELECTIONS MORE THAN ONCE

If you have been preparing an Easter work, or are already thinking about your Christmas work, why save all the music and sing it on the one big night!?!? Why not consider, several weeks out, allowing the congregation to begin hearing and becoming familiar with some of the music the choir will be singing?

The choir members get to have the music for many weeks, during which they learn to love and appreciate it. The poor congregation only hears it once, and we wonder why they don't 'get it'. One hearing is never enough.

You can use portions of the major production music as calls to worship, anthems, or benedictions. The congregation will enjoy hearing it more than once, and just as the choir enjoys singing the pieces many times over to get it just right, the congregation will enjoy hearing the pieces at least twice!

67 MYSTERY CHOIR OR INSTRUMENTAL MEMBER OF THE WEEK

If you have a choir paper, you might consider having a "Mystery Choir Member of the Week." You gather a few facts, mostly true ones, give enough clues to make it almost impossible to guess, and give a nice prize for the first one who guesses who the person is. The prize could be one of the following:

- A 'seat of honor' during the next choir rehearsal, right next to the conductor
- Someone to hold and turn the music during rehearsal for the winner
- A CD or cassette from the many you receive each week and would love to give away
- Someone to hang up the choir robe for the winner after Sunday's service
- A solo in an upcoming worship service in the year 2010
- The privilege to baby-sit the choir director's children on the night of their choice
- The chance to take the director to lunch next week, and pay
- Any other prize you can imagine

68 PERFORM CHRISTMAS MUSIC OUTSIDE THE CHURCH

Consider taking your Christmas program, or a portion of that program 'on the road' – to a mission or community church, a elderly rest home, a children's hospital, the local airport, or some other place in your community that would be open to such an exciting event. The performance will do several things for you and your choir:

1 • Provide opportunity for a 'dry run' to see if everything is ready

2 • Provide inspiration to those who listen

3 • Provide inspiration to those who will sing

4 • Present an opportunity for ministry and missions

5 • Give those participating an opportunity to get outside the walls of the church and experience the 'real' world

69 PIGGYBACK ON A HERO

When you discover that someone you respect and admire is going to be in or near your city, figure out how you can secure his or her services for your church family or ministry. If, for instance, you live in Orlando, and Christine Anderson is going to be there for a bell festival, try to have her come in early or stay later and do a one-evening bell seminar with your ringers. If Randy Edwards is coming near your city for a YouthCUE event, contact him in advance, tell him what you have in mind, quote an honorarium fee and tell him you'll pay any extra expenses, and you'll probably have him with your group!

This kind of piggyback scheduling is good for you, because you don't have to pay full airfare or major travel expenses. It is good for the clinician because he or she has opportunities to teach, train and inspire as well as getting an extra day or two of honorarium. I used to do this frequently in the local church.

A word of caution: Don't take the position that you already gleaned all you can from a guest and use that as an excuse to skip the major event that brought him or her to town in the first place! That undermines the program. Use the person as the opportunity for extra teaching, training and inspiration before or after the major event.

70 PLAN TO SPEND EXTRA TIME WITH FAMILY THIS FALL

PLAN TO DO SPECIAL THINGS ALONG THE WAY WITH SPOUSE AND KIDS. IT WILL PAY OFF IN THE END.

The downward spiral toward Christmas has begun! Many of us are already involved in Christmas projects such as regularly scheduled rehearsals, set design, costuming, planning extra rehearsal times, and much more!

Christmas is such a wonderful and delightful time and it should forever remain that way, even in the midst of 'too much to do and too little time to do it!' I highly recommend spending extra time with spouse and children during these pressure times. Remember: in the intense season that is upon us, the tendency will be to go to work early and stay late, to work on weekends and days off. And guess who gets the brunt of a spouse too involved in ministry, with too little sleep, too little exercise and too much time spent at the church? Right: *the family!* So…covenant to make this season a jolly one and plan to do special things along the way with spouse and kids. It will pay off in the end, guaranteed!

71 POPCORN & PILLOWS

Consider having a popcorn and pillows rehearsal! I know, it sounds strange, but it really works! If you would like to have the whole choir listen to the new Christmas or Easter production music, with scores in hand, announce a popcorn and pillows rehearsal.

Ask the choir members to bring to the next rehearsal their favorite pillow(s), large and/or small. Have an old-time popcorn machine going as they enter the rehearsal area, the smell will be a wonderful 'welcome' to the choir room. Have plenty of soft drinks, juice, water and coffee available. Have plenty of napkins, too. Clear the choir room of all chairs, move the piano against the wall.

As the choir members enter, let them find a favorite spot and get comfortable with popcorn and drinks. Make appropriate comments about the work, including the concept of the work, the composer and/or lyricist, and what plans you have for the production. Have a session of prayer and then begin a CD recording of the work, with a good sound system, good speakers, and good volume. You can stop at appropriate places in the work for further explanation, if necessary.

When the recording is finished, have everyone help with the cleanup process from popcorn fights and other mischief! Of course, you'll need to have a sugar-stick anthem ready for Sunday, as little rehearsal on upcoming music will be done. The choir will have had a great time with the three L's: laughing, listening, and learning the work. And this is a fun way to get two things accomplished: fellowship and a good listening of a new work!

72 SEVEN HINTS FOR FOLLOWING LEADERS

1. USE OBSTACLES TO YOUR ADVANTAGE
2. STAY TRUE TO YOUR VISION
3. CREATE YOUR OWN OPPORTUNITIES
4. THINK BIG; DREAM THE DREAM
5. FIND YOUR OWN SOLUTIONS
6. TREAT THOSE AROUND YOU AS A RESOURCE
7. CHALLENGE THE STATUS QUO

73 SEVEN HINTS FOR LEADING FOLLOWERS

USE OBSTACLES TO YOUR ADVANTAGE 1

Do not give in or give up easily.

STAY TRUE TO YOUR VISION 2

Without a vision, there is no leadership!

CREATE YOUR OWN OPPORTUNITIES 3

No one else will create them for you.

THINK BIG; DREAM THE DREAM 4

Bigger than those you lead.

FIND YOUR OWN SOLUTIONS 5

Good solutions take thought, energy and fortitude.

TREAT THOSE AROUND YOU AS A RESOURCE 6

People will be willing to help and assist if they feel appreciated and feel as if they are accomplishing something in the process.

CHALLENGE THE STATUS QUO 7

Never accept what is. Always look for what can be!

74 SIGNS YOUR LEADERSHIP STYLE IS IN TROUBLE

First comes the thunder,
then comes the lightning,
and then comes the storm.

First comes the sniffles,
then comes the cold.

First comes the noise
and then comes the flat tire.

Warning signs are wonderful things because they do just that: warn us of approaching trouble. There are warning signs, too, in smaller church music leadership responsibilities. Here are a few:

People have stopped coming to rehearsals.

An old cowboy saying: "When you are riding out in front of the herd, look back ever so often to see if they are still following you." This is especially true in leadership. You can get so far ahead (or behind) of your fellowship that they give up on you! You may be doing so much they can't keep up and become discouraged. You may be doing too little, not challenging the choir and leading them to say say, "Why bother!" Ever so often, place a sheet of colored paper in every rehearsal chair with a pencil. Let your people become acquainted with the idea that when they see that color paper, they have the freedom to write you a personal note, no holds barred, and you will learn a lot! Trust them, they aren't usually wrong.

People seem to be complaining all the time.

What are they complaining about? Listen carefully to them. Are there too many new hymns/choruses? Are you singing the same old-same old week after week after month? Is rehearsal boring? Is the worship service boring because it never changes? Do you sing the same music over and over and over? Are you too aloof from the choir members, not spending time with them? Do you pop in just in time for rehearsal and then pop out and are gone? Listen to your people.

Your other job is taking so much of your time...

...that you don't have any quality time to plan worship, learn new music, be with people, and/or attend any conferences to better your musicianship. If you answered yes, you must decide if you should step down and let someone else have a turn at the thrill of music leadership. Don't hang on just because you've always done it! There may be a better person capable of leading the rehearsal and the service, right in front of you, and you never thought about it. Well, think about it. It might be time for a change!

Read the signs!

75 STRESS REDUCERS

You know it! I know it! Everyone knows it! There is a lot of stress coming during these next weeks, whether we like it or not! The preparations, rehearsals, and all the extra things that have to happen when Christmas productions are looming in front of us will certainly give stress. It will happen!!

Try any or all of the following as often as possible to reduce stress:

Always get a good night's sleep

As you prepare the day, pray for spiritual guidance

Always eat a good breakfast

Prepare for today the night before

Write a love note to someone

Cut out caffeine

Laugh often

Read something funny and inspirational each day

Sing a happy song

Look out the window often

Avoid negative people

Take a brisk walk with a friend or your spouse

Count to 100 and wait 3 days before reacting to a bad situation

Play racquetball or tennis

Count your blessings

Go to lunch with a dear friend

Learn to say no

Quit trying to 'fix' things for other people

Don't expect people to read your mind!

Laugh…play…pray

Don't procrastinate; get organized.

Apologize for a mistake

Lighten up; stress can be beaten!

Be more forgiving of others, and yourself

Always look your best

Don't slump; walk tall and proud

Exercise, stretch

Give honest praise to someone each day

76 SUCCESSFUL PEOPLE ARE HAPPY!

No matter the job title or age, true success requires this, at least: Be happy! No matter what other goals they may have, truly successful people enjoy every day, and take time to laugh and love. Here are 4 suggestions of happy, successful people:

1 You can be happy any time you wish! Happiness is a choice. Laugh, have fun, lighten up! You can do it now, and it is free!

2 Keep a gratitude journal. Every day, take a moment to list the things that bring you joy. Notice the people and opportunities that make you thankful. Write them down! When you get a chance, tell the people in your life that you love and appreciate them!

3 Work less, spend less, need less. Simplify life until it feels manageable again. You can't have it all anyway, so choose the things that are worth working for.

4 Don't sweat the small stuff, and it's all small stuff! We panic over petty things. We worry about stuff that never happens. Why do we do this? Life is short...enjoy it!

Happiness is about living a life that is consistent with our highest values.

Happiness is about taking time, fulfilling a dream, being grateful, or being with people we love and respect.

Happiness is not a mysterious, mystical, impossible dream.

Happiness is about smelling the roses.

Is it easy to be happy? Judging from the folks we see around us and read about in the paper every day, apparently not. Is it something you can achieve? Absolutely! Why not decide to be different? Be happy!

77 TAKE THIS QUIZ

1. Name the five wealthiest people in the world.
2. Name the last five Heisman-trophy winners.
3. Name the last five winners of the Miss America Beauty Pageant.
4. Name ten people who have won the Nobel Prize or Pulitzer Prize.
5. Name the last six Academy Award winners for best actor/actress.
6. Name the last ten World Series winners.

How did you do? You failed, didn't you? The point is this: most of us do not remember the headliners of yesterday (and these were no second-rate achievers). These people were the best in their fields,

MORE

but applause dies. Awards tarnish. Achievements are forgotten. Accolades and certificates are buried with their owners.

Here's another quiz. See how you do on this one:

1. List the teacher who most influenced your journey through school.
2. Name three friends who have helped you through a difficult time.
3. Name five people who have taught you something worthwhile
4. Name two who have made you feel appreciated and special.
5. Name five people with whom you enjoy spending time.
6. Name six heroes in your personal journey.

Was this an easier quiz? The lesson? The people who make a difference in your life are not those with the most credentials, the most money, or the most awards. They are those who care. It's as simple as that!

78 TEN PRINCIPLES FOR MINISTRY CHARACTER DEVELOPMENT

by Bill Wilson, Director/Founder of Metro Ministries International, Brooklyn, New York

1. Build on your strengths.
2. Do not get involved with fools.
3. To be is more important then to do.
4. The good always has been and always will be the enemy of the best.
5. You will only be remembered for two things in your life: (1) the problems you solve and (2) the problems you create.
6. What happens in you is more important that what happens to you.
7. You cannot unscramble eggs.
8. When you get something you have never had, you become responsible for doing something you have never done.
9. If people don't know your passion, you don't have any!
10. Being faithful is more important than being successful.

79 TEN THINGS TO LEARN FROM CRITICISM

As you go into a Christmas season, be aware that criticism can and probably will, abound. Comments such as: The music is too loud. The music is too soft. There were too many instruments. There were not enough instruments. Why didn't you do this? Why didn't you do that? Out of all criticism can come positive learning experiences if you:

KEEP YOUR PERSPECTIVE

Keep in mind what God has called you to be and do.

BE HONEST

Ask yourself: Perhaps, is the critic right? If so, change what needs to be changed. Your critic has helped you.

LEARN FROM CRITICISM

It's dangerous to think every critic is wrong. God may be saying something to you through this experience. Listen carefully and constructively.

MOVE ON IF YOU FEEL THE CRITICISM IS UNFOUNDED

Never feel you must argue or retaliate.

REMEMBER YOU AND YOUR CRITIC ARE PROBABLY PURSUING THE SAME GOAL

Some of the severest critics are good people who want to see the work of God progress as much as you do.

REMEMBER THAT THE CRITIC

...may be expressing unprocessed anger or personal failure.

DON'T DWELL ON THE NEGATIVE

Take strength from all the positive people in your life, most especially your family.

STAY IN GOD'S WORD

In difficult times, make sure your personal devotional time is sharp and focused.

ENCOURAGE OTHERS

When you lift another, you are lifted in the process.

REMEMBER WHO THE ULTIMATE AUDIENCE OF SIGNIFICANCE IS: GOD

He has the final word on your efforts in ministry.

Now, develop a Christ-like spirit and listen to criticism, but don't respond. Take what you feel is good and discard the rest. Get on with your life!

80 TEN WAYS TO EARN STAFF RESPECT, AND THE CONFIDENCE OF A PASTOR

1

RESPECT YOURSELF Know your strengths and weaknesses.

2

GIVE CREDIT WHERE IT IS DUE Be lavish in giving away applause to others.

3

DON'T BE TOO FAMILIAR WITH YOUR PEOPLE We all want to be loved and appreciated. Just be careful and very wise.

4

CRITICIZE IN PRIVATE Commend in public.

5

OBSERVE ALL THE RULES YOU EXPECT EVERYONE ELSE TO OBSERVE

6

DON'T MAKE PROMISES YOU CAN'T FULFILL

7

RESPECT CONFIDENCES Keep it to yourself.

8

BE CONSISTENT Don't be moody and don't give your personal burdens to others. They have enough of their own.

9

KEEP CALM UNDER THE MOST TRYING OF CIRCUMSTANCES We all want to run and hide but we can't. Show confidence and people will catch it — and want it.

10

SHOW ENTHUSIASM AND JOY IN YOUR JOB Delight in your position. Enjoy your people. Make the most and the best of every situation.

81 THANK YOU

Bob Briner, in his book, *Men In Leadership* (Broadman & Holman), makes this statement on "Day 21":

> *"Good leaders understand that they don't need to do it all, really cannot do it all, and even it they could do it all, they shouldn't! Quality leaders understand that a team effort is always better than one person doing it all."*

Along with those words, Briner also says:

> *"Thank-you notes should be a staple on your desk or in your briefcase, so that any moment, you can jot a quick word of gratitude to someone who deserves it!"*

You've heard it said from this writer that "You can't appreciate people too much!" That is so very true, yet many church leaders and church musicians never bother to let their people know how much they are appreciated! You would be amazed to see how your people will respond to a thank-you note written by you for something they did well! It will go a long way, I assure you. Never underestimate the power of a thank-you note.

82 THE MORE PEOPLE YOU INVOLVE TO HELP YOU...

...the stronger your support base will become! I know ministers of music who try to do it all, everything, the whole enchilada, and I know their ministry will be severely hampered because only one person is involved, and one person doing all the work!

People want to help and assist. People *want* to be asked to be a part of something that is worth their time and effort. People *want* to serve and be productive. People *want* to be made to feel important and what they are doing is worthwhile. The load is easier to carry if three or fifteen are helping do the task. There are people in your choir program who are just waiting to be asked to serve...and they will astound you with what they are capable of doing when unleashed and turned loose to do it.

You can't do it all, nor should you! Get some help!

83 THREE RULES FOR SUCCESS

Clear blueprints Numbers and dates and costs and measurements that give you the focus for peak performance. Success is the result of a well-defined goal and clear, workable plans for achievement. Spend time designing well! Think about what you want, talk with experts, read and take notes. The first principle for success: Know your outcome!

Environmental fitness 'Time management' is no longer. Time just is. To achieve success, we must manage ourselves and the world around us. Work to make it easy to reach your goal. Winners have clean offices, the best equipment and clear schedules. When your environment makes success easy, you'll win every time!

Support systems. Fill your life with people who encourage you, and learn from people who have achieved what you want to achieve. There's an old saying, "It's hard to soar with the eagles when you're scratching with turkeys." Surround yourself with cheerleaders, coaches, mentors, models, and team members who are committed to your success. Remember: success is a team activity. Get a coach or mentor who believes in you, and is determined to take you to the top! Teach your friends and family the best ways to encourage you. Fill your life with winners because success breeds success!

TIME 84

Time is the new currency of the 21st century. The new poverty is time starvation! With these thoughts in mind, how are you handling the time God has given you, 24 hours in a day?

A good check list of the time you spend each week would be to keep a time sheet, like you used to do in college. Begin on Monday, and put down everything you do in the week, with the time allotted. When you finish, you will be amazed at what you discover.

How much quality time

did you spend with your spouse?
did you spend with your children?

How much actual time

did you use planning and preparing the worship service for God's people?

How much time did you spend

in preparation for your main rehearsals?
taking care of your health?
dreaming and creating?
in spiritual and musical preparation for each rehearsal?
in prayer?
affirming, loving and supporting your church and choir people?

My! Where did the time go?

TIME: USE IT WISELY 85

Each of us has the same amount of time: 24/7/365. No one can change that. No one has ever had more, or less time! Everyone has the same amount. What you do with your time takes careful and thoughtful planning. Time is the currency of the 21st century. People no longer ask, "How much will this cost?" they ask, "How much time will this take?" Time becomes even more valuable in two arenas:

Personal growth and maturity For us to continue to grow spiritually, relationally, musically and in favor with God and man, we must make room for personal growth. Maturing will soon follow. In this day and age, we can no longer afford to be concerned with just our own personal ministry, however large or small it may be. We must be concerned with the larger arena of personal discipline and development. You can only get this by making time for it in your life.

Musical and spiritual development You can no longer be the musician you were even ten years ago. Music has changed, even if you have not. Today's music requires personal study and discipline to ensure that you get every nugget from the score. You can no longer treat your choir(s) the same as you did ten years ago. Time has made a major impact on attendance and unless you are offering something in rehearsals that is more appealing than staying home or going somewhere more fun or disciplined, your average attendance is probably falling! If you are not in God's Word daily, if you are not praying constantly, if you are not mentoring someone and being mentored yourself, if you are not communicating with fellow musicians, if you are not going to conferences and finding times of training, you are becoming average, and there are too many average people out there today who are making no difference in the Kingdom.

Don't be average. Use your time wisely.

86 TWELVE COMPETENCIES OF CHRISTIAN LEADERSHIP

by Barna Research Group, Ltd., Ventura, California

1. Identifies, articulates, and attempts to follow God's call on his or her life.
2. Coaches and develops leaders – a must for the future.
3. Develops and communicates strategies, makes plans for the future.
4. Motivates people to become involved. Realizes he or she can't do it all by him or herself.
5. Efficiently mobilizes ministry participants, has good working teams.
6. Able to resolve conflict, personal and job-related.
7. Identifies and acquires needed resources, keeps abreast and aware.
8. Reinforces commitment and success, strives for the best quality.
9. Objectively evaluates ministry often; how are things?
10. Intentionally shapes the culture where he or she is serving, aims for the best.
11. Models Christian character and commitment. Character is never in question.
12. Attracts and maintains an effective team. Works hard to keep the best people.

87 VALUE SKILLS

In a recent survey, people were asked to give their opinion of the top 'value skill' of leadership. Here are the results:

This seems to always be a concern for leadership, good leaders are honest!

HONESTY

Leaders have moral and spiritual integrity.

INTEGRITY

If the leader is not totally on board, how can others be expected to be committed?

COMMITMENT

Will the leader 'go to the wall' for the project or presentation?

LOYALTY

How truly fair are our leaders in all venues of responsibilities?

FAIRNESS

Is there a real interest and concern for his or her followers?

CONCERN FOR OTHERS

Does the leader have genuine respect for those whom he or she is leading? If not, why?

RESPECT

Does the leader bend all of the rules to suit him or herself?

OBEDIENCE TO THE LAW

Is excellence a part of the fiber of the being of the leader?

PURSUIT OF EXCELLENCE

Without this, a leader is leading no one but him or herself.

PERSONAL ACCOUNTABILITY

88 VISIBILITY – WHEN AND WHERE

Effective leaders understand the value of appropriate visibility. The 'isolationist leader' is probably a contradiction in terms. Good leaders know how to stay close to the action. A good example is **Sir Winston Churchill,** whose war strategy included placing military leaders on the front lines. He personally showed up in the most dangerous places in

London during WWII. The modern Israeli army, one of the most formidable military forces in the world, has adopted Churchill's suggestions.

When **Lee Iacocca** assumed leadership of Chrysler, the company was on the brink of ruin. His first action was to aggressively interact with workers, generating a 'winner attitude'. Many believe that his high visibility was the most important element in his leadership.

In a recent study of effective leaders, **George Barna** found this attribute of visibility to be present in all of them. While the effective leader did not necessarily seek the spotlight, effective leaders always seemed to be in the right place, at the right time, for the right reasons. They appear to have the ability to remain in focus without being the focus of the church. They have their fingers on the pulse of the situation and can determine where their presence would be most effective.

Effective leaders, who carry influence, just know which occasions they should attend (or miss) and they know exactly when to arrive to those events they choose to attend. They know when to write a special note or make a phone call or pay a visit. And it's all accomplished through a lot of prayer, intuition, and good 'horse sense'.

89 VISIT ALL MUSIC MINISTRY GROUPS OFTEN

Just show up and 'love on' the leadership and those involved.

That's right!

If you are not very careful, you will find yourself interested in and concerned only with the groups for which you are the conductor. The members of those other choirs and ensembles that are run by some else rarely, if ever, see you in person, except in the pulpit.

Visit each of the graded choir rehearsals at least once a month. Dropping in and saying hello will encourage your faithful workers. Let them see you outside of 'big church'! Visit vocal, instrumental, and handbell ensembles, letting them know of your personal and musical support. You don't have to stay long, and you don't have to conduct or even given musical advice or critique!

You will begin to discover that all involved will have a new appreciation for you and your interest in them. This goes a long, long way in today's society.

Choir Officers and Their Responsibilities

90 A MAKE OVER

Have you ever thought about having a make over!?!? No! Not for you, but for your rehearsal suite or room! Most rehearsal suites/rooms are dull, boring, lifeless and totally uninteresting. Changes are rare. The pictures or posters probably have not been refreshed since 1969! Christmas decorations or remnants of last Easter may still be sitting in the corners. Music is everywhere, yet in its proper place. Chairs may be in disarray. Know the scene?

Well, isn't it about time to freshen-up the rehearsal room?

Consider having it thoroughly cleaned: sweep, polish, deep clean the carpet, and make everything shiny! How about some helium balloons tied to 10 or 20 chairs throughout the choir room on rehearsal night? Use lots of string so the balloons will be high in the air. The choir members will enjoy this, I assure you. New posters or pictures would be a good addition. Be creative. Think how you could do a little fixing-up and please your members for the new year! You'll be glad you did.

P. S. This is a good job for the choir officers, who would do a good job with this assignment!

91 AN ATTRACTIVE REHEARSAL ROOM...

...is important to current members, but it is also very necessary in attracting new members and welcoming visitors. How long has it been since you made any changes in your rehearsal room – moving chairs, changing the bulletin board, making sure the floor is clean, or even something as simple as room freshener?

Your people spend quite a bit of time in the rehearsal room, and the room should be made as attractive and inviting as possible. Once in a while, balloons tied to the chairs will bring freshness to the room. Colorful streamers around the room have the same effect. Maybe place Snickers bars on the chairs, or how about making sure the chairs are straight and ready for the choir members?

Rehearsal rooms can be depressing. Is yours? If so, get a committee and put them to work. Assign them the task of brightening up the rehearsal area (or do it yourself) and surprise the choir next week. You will get comments, most of them positive!

92 CHANGE THAT REHEARSAL SUITE AROUND

Who said everything must and should remain the same!?!? One of the best places to begin to experiment with change is the rehearsal suite/room. If you are fortunate enough to have one, bless God. Someone told me recently that he has to rehearse in the Fellowship Hall and can't set the room till *after Wednesday night suppers!* How sad, but the church is growing and it is the best they can do right now!

If you have a rehearsal room, look around and consider ways to change it, brighten it up, clean it up, and have a few surprises for the next rehearsal. One good surprise is to turn the room around! Now if you have permanent risers, this is of course impossible, but if the choir is on floor level, turn it around, get eyes away from the point of entry, focus their attention on the conductor. You'll find a new zeal of attention on you, the conductor!

93 CHOIR CELEBRATIONS

from Church Music In Today's World, *by Bob Burroughs, © 2001 by Tempo Music, used by permission*

Many times, choir rehearsals can be boring, because no one ever has any fun, especially the director! There is little excitement in the room! Everyone is way too serious, and there is little creativity in the room. You and your choir officers can create fun surprises and events that will make the choir members excited and happy about being in the rehearsal. You can make the choir room, the people, and the robe rooms all come alive with 'phun, phood, phellowship', and good feelings about each other, the choir, and the church!

By the way, one of the most boring rooms in the church is the choir room! This room – of all rooms – should be bright, and happy, with balloons and streamers, because in this room are the most creative people in the church! Here are some ideas for the Choir Year that might get your creative juices flowing for times of celebration with your choir:

JANUARY

New Choir-Year Party the first rehearsal back from Christmas.

FEBRUARY

Valentine Party or Banquet. This can be as simple as an after-choir snack with finger foods.

MARCH

St. Patrick's Day (of course, everyone is required to wear green). Or how about a Welcome to Spring Party?

APRIL
April Fool's Day, obviously! Have a 'backwards party' and turn the choir room completely around. Have surprises.

MAY
End-of-School Party or an End-of-Choir Banquet. Be sure to hold it at a special place.

JUNE
Welcome to Summer Party. This is a great enlistment time for summer semester!

JULY
4th-of-July Celebration with a red, white and blue theme, or have a Baseball Party.

AUGUST
End-of-Summer Banquet; Composer's Weekend Banquet; Music Ministry Banquet; or, even better, August Off – No Rehearsals!

SEPTEMBER
Back-to-School Party or a Back-to-Choir Party.

OCTOBER
Welcome-to-Fall Party or a Halloween Celebration, with everyone coming to choir in costumes. Give prizes!

NOVEMBER
Thanksgiving Celebration. Do something nice, as a choir, for a needy family.

DECEMBER
Christmas Party, what else.

94 CONSIDER CHRISTMAS LUMINARIES

Yes, consider surrounding your church's main entrance with luminaries: bags with sand in the bottom and a small candle in each bag. These lighted bags can be lining the walks into the sanctuary for each evening Christmas program. They will create a great deal of excitement around your church, both with the membership and from passing motorists, too.

Be sure to check the local fire codes first and secure responsible people to manage this project. This is a good youth or young-adult project, and they will love doing it. You'll be glad you did this.

95 EASTER? *ALREADY?*

Yes, it is past time to think of the Easter programming, but it's not too late. Think of something new, original and creative to do this next season. Don't always rely on the same old same old. Challenge your singers and instrumentalists with a new venture. Combine the classical and contemporary, do some of both. Be sure to 'take your program on the road' and try it out on a smaller church or a mission. The selected church, as well as your choir/orchestra, will be the better for the adventure. Plan now where you can go to minister and sing.

Also, just a thought: consider if multiple performances are really necessary, and whether these extra performances are for Him or for your ego. Consider what it does to the family unit to have performances for 3-8 nights in a row, or even several weekends in a row!

96 END-OF-THE-YEAR CELEBRATION

Thought about closing out the Spring semester with your adult choir in a special way? It is a good thing to bring closure to each season. This can be done as elaborately or as simply as you have time, money and effort. Here are some suggestions:

1. A banquet recognizing everyone. Give certificates. Have a speaker.

2. Host a party at someone's home. Maybe a barbeque, with all the trimmings.

3. Throw a party in the choir room during final week. Instead of rehearsal, surprise the choir with finger foods, drinks and goodies. Let them visit and share their most favorite choir experience. You will learn loads!

Makes no difference what you do, just do something! The choir will love it!

97 IF SOMEONE NEW TO YOUR CHURCH WAS TO ENTER YOUR CHOIR ROOM...

...Would they be welcomed immediately, by someone other than the director, who would take them 'under their wing', introduce them to others in their vocal section, get them the evening's music packet or copies of the music, answer the questions that might came up, and made to feel comfortable in the rehearsal setting?

If the answer was no to any of these statements, you might realize why your choir membership isn't growing! A choir can be a 'closed community' unless you work hard at keeping the choir aware of new people and how to make them feel comfortable. This is key to successful recruiting.

98 LOOK UNDER THE CHAIR

A great way to keep your rehearsals interesting and your choir members alert and guessing is to periodically hide something under certain chairs in random fashion. Tape M&M's, a candy bar, bubble gum, Life-Savers, or anything available under the chairs. You know all those cassettes and CDs of musicals or anthems that publishers send out? After you hear them and they begin to stack up, tape them under the chairs. Choir members will be thrilled to have a new cassette or CD, regardless of what it is! You can also create little homemade things to be placed under the chairs, such as notes that say things like:

This note allows you to have someone hold your folder during rehearsal next week.

This note gives you the privilege of one musical error without comment from the director. Just show it when you sing the wrong note or enter wrong.

This note provides you assistance in robing next Sunday.

This note allows you to tell one joke during next week's rehearsal. By the way, there is no rehearsal next week!

You can make up a whole host of things. At a certain moment in the rehearsal, tell the choir members to look under their chairs for a surprise. Everyone will enjoy looking and finding something and those who don't can anticipate next week. Once in a while, put something under every chair! This is a great job for choir officers.

99 NEW YEAR CHOIR/INSTRUMENTAL KICKOFF

I know, Christmas isn't over yet, but you should be thinking about a kick off for the new music year! Why??

! Because to do a kickoff properly will take some planning and creative time.

! Because it a time to begin anew and to start over.

! Because it is right around the corner.

! Because you'll want to do some things differently in this new year.

! Because the members will come expecting something exciting to happen.

! Because you want to give your people the best possible rehearsal experiences.

! Because there are still people in your congregation who should be singing in the choir or playing in the instrumental ensemble.

Plan, carry out, promote, encourage. You'll have a great new year!

100 PLAN FOR THE NEW YEAR, AND FOR THE FUTURE

There are those in music ministry (and some even in pastoral ministry) who do zero-to-little planning beyond what is absolutely necessary or required! These kinds of people just barely get by week-to-week! I trust you are not one of those! Advance planning, especially in this day and age, is absolutely necessary in order to have a successful program and ministry, or to be successful yourself! You must know very clearly where you are right now, decide where you would like to be now, or where you would like your program to be within a certain time frame, and then work very hard to reach your goal(s). I've always tried to work with ten-year goals, which always seemed logical to me.

A good question to ask yourself as this new year begins is this: "Where would I like to be in ten years?"

Remember that things, and situations, will change and so will you! So be it. But at least, you should begin the thinking/planning process. The beginning of a new year is a great time for reflection, dreaming, and planning. It is a time to review your progress, examine your choices, make new commitments, and review old ones to see if they are still worth your time.

It might be time to decide what you want to do with the rest of your life! If you really wish to secure a higher education degree, you can do it. Yes, it will take some expert planning/time commitments, but it can be done. These days, a bachelor's degree is not enough. There is a whole world of expertise out there in the 'real world' and this degree just scratches the surface. Don't let anyone tell you that you have 'enough' education. You don't! None of us do!

There is always something new to learn – about yourself, your job, about worship, your church, your pastor, your people, music, life, how to do things better/simpler, your marriage, your children – and you won't learn if you are willing to just slide by from day-to-day, week-to-week, month-to-month and year-to-year without thinking into the future! So…plan, dream, think, and you'll be surprised what the Lord will bring to your subconscious mind for pondering!

101 READY OR NOT…FALL IS HERE

Fall, that great time of the year when the leaves begin to show their colors, the days get a bit shorter, college and pro football teams begin to challenge each other, and choir and orchestra activities kick in afresh and anew! Are you ready? If not, you had better begin planning now! Here are some suggestions:

MORE

Begin to contact
your choir/orchestra members *now*, by email, post card, letter, or, better yet, some fun, exciting, creative, and adventurous way to get their attention and make your point.

Promote, promote, promote.
And then, promote some more.

Have Choir/Orchestra Open House
or Guest Night at the first rehearsal. Have key people ready to host, mentor, introduce, and walk visitors through the process of 'choir'. Remember: the choir room is a very intimidating place for a new comer.

Put flyers on the windshields
of every car in the parking lot on a given Sunday, telling about the Fall Choir/Instrumental Programs

Establish a phone bank
Have choir members call new prospects for choir/orchestra often, providing them with a 'tip' for Fall.

These are just a few ideas, you can come up with others, but time is fleeting! Remember: it takes the average person 11 times before something he or she heard or saw will stick in the memory.

102 REFRESH YOUR REHEARSAL ROOM

This is a great time to gather your officers together and plan a day in the summer to refurbish and refresh the rehearsal area. It probably needs it. ***Rehearsal rooms are usually the most boring places in the church,*** with chairs in disarray, litter and dust everywhere, bulletin boards that haven't been updated since May 12, 1954, and no bright color within view.

Change all that!

Find ways to brighten the room: fresh paint, new pictures, and a good cleaning that includes polishing the chairs, floor, piano, and robe rooms. Let your imagination run free! You and the officers will find your rehearsal room a much more enjoyable place to work, and so will the members!

103

SEATING CAPTAIN

Do you have trouble seating and/or lining up the choir or ensemble every Sunday? With limited time already making it hard to run through the music, are you stressed trying to get the choir ready to go out into the choir loft as more late comers enter, wondering where they should sit?

Why not consider selecting a strong and faithful (faithful is the key word here) person with a strong personality and ask him or her to be the seating captain!? While you are rehearsing and giving last-minute music or worship instructions, this person can be moving people here and there, counting chairs, filling spaces, and making the set-up look right. This person should be of a personality that will not to take any guff, and certainly not a person that can have his or her feelings hurt easily. This person should be 'in charge' during this time. The choir should be told in advance that this person will do this task on a regular basis and that they should cooperate — and anyone who doesn't will have their robe burned next Wednesday night after rehearsal! This idea works — it really works — and the choir members will be happy that someone is taking over this responsibility for you, the conductor!

104

SIX-MONTH TERM FOR CHOIR OFFICERS

As strange at it may seem, choir officers usually lose interest in their positions if they last longer than six months. Choirs that elect officers for one year usually get about six months of work out of these people, and the end result is an officer position that lacks leadership for the remaining six months. There is generally an excitement among the choir officers when their term of office runs from January through June or July through December, because they do not have a full-year term with which to be concerned. After six months, they can get on with their lives. Try it once, and you will never go back to the old way of one-year terms. Sounds like a prison sentence, doesn't it? Sometimes, it is! Try the six-month officers, you – and the choir – will be pleased. Experiment with January to June and July to December.

105 THE FUTURE IS HERE NOW

The future is here — ready or not! And you know, sometimes we get so caught up in little things that are so unimportant that we forget the things that really count. We often tend to major on minor things and minor on major things. What are, or should be, the 'major things' in your life?

Ideas for 'major things' thinking include:

A
Pray often with your spouse and your children.

B
Scripture readings and devotionals will benefit the family.

C
Keep sharp and up-to-date in your chosen ministry area.

D
Always be learning, seeking new ideas and ways to do your job better.

E
Write notes of gratitude and thanksgiving to those you love and appreciate. Remember – you can't appreciate people enough.

F
Never pass up an opportunity to explore and renew conducting, keyboard, instrumental or vocal skills.

G
Never be satisfied with where you are in life, always seek God's leadership to stretch yourself and your family.

H
Never be satisfied with just a bachelor's degree when there are ways and opportunities for higher education degrees available today.

I
Establish annuities or funds for the future. Retirement will come sooner rather than later.

J
Begin saving now for the kid's education and/or wedding. Remember: $50 a month, saved for 20 years, at 9% interest, will provide over $75,000. Everyone can afford $50 a month!

Have you ever made out your 'major things' list? Perhaps this would be a good week to do it.

106 WELCOME TO THE PARTY

Everyone loves a good party. Music people especially like a good party, but they don't come too often due to scheduling and time management. Why not consider kicking off your first rehearsal with a big 'Welcome to the Party' party? Decorate the choir room with a special theme, have balloons around, decorate the walls with theme posters, serve unusual things to snack on. Have the choir folders loaded with the new music. Let them fellowship for 15 minutes, then get into a good, well-paced rehearsal, continuing to use party-theme words to keep the interest up. This will take a bit of creativity, but the event will be appreciated by those who attend. Good promotion will help! Plan ahead!

Choir Members

107 A BLANK SHEET OF PAPER...

...can be placed on every choir or orchestra chair on a given rehearsal night and, at some point in the rehearsal, the leader simply says:

> *"You were given a blank sheet of paper tonight. I am interested in hearing from you. You can write me a note telling me anything you wish and I'll respond accordingly. You can encourage or complain. You can rant, rave or give me a suggestion or two. You can write this anytime this week and leave it on my desk, send it by mail, and you don't even have to sign it! I'm interested in hearing from you."*

You will be amazed at the response you will receive. This should be done every six months or so, and soon, the choir/orchestra will begin to look forward to communicating with you in this manner.

108 A CHRISTMAS SURPRISE

Why not consider doing something really special and unusual during one of the upcoming Christmas rehearsals? This special or unusual event could be one of the following ideas:

▲ *Invite a special surprise guest or well-known local inspirational speaker to bring a devotional word.*

▲ *Ask your pastor to drop-in during the middle of a rehearsal for a quick thought or inspirational comment.*

▲ *Ask someone the choir really respects from outside the church to visit a rehearsal and bring a critique of what he or she sees and hears. It will certainly put them on their best behavior and encourage them to sing and play better.*

▲ *At one of the final rehearsals, secretly invite all the wives, husbands, children, and grandchildren to come to the rehearsal as 'special guests'. Recognize them before rehearsal begins and honor them for the many hours you have taken from their family time. Shower them with gifts: flowers, candy, VIP nametags, etc.*

▲ *Quit rehearsal early, for once, and let the people go home ahead of time. They will be in shock!*

▲ *Put certain color dots on rehearsal folders and, between songs, announce prizes for those with a certain color dot. See if you can't get business in the community to donate the prizes.*

▲ *You can think of other grand things to do. Just do it! Remember: you are asking for many hours of their time, so be creative and make them feel really special during those long rehearsals and preparations!*

▲ *Have the Baskin-Robbins Ice Cream people show up with a couple of containers of ice cream, with cones, scoops and napkins. At the end of a long rehearsal, give everyone a big double dip.*

▲ *Ask Santa to come and interrupt a rehearsal for a nice break. Let him give everyone a gift, from you.*

109 CHOIR/INSTRUMENTAL MENTORS

Choir or orchestra can be, and usually is, a very intimidating place! To walk into a room where everyone knows everyone, and you know no one, is very difficult. That's why every group needs to have ensemble mentors: selected people who can and are willing to 'shepherd' new recruits into the ensemble family. These people are assigned to new members, they sit with them in rehearsal, help them learn the ropes of how things are done in the choir, like where to get music, pencils, and robes. Mentors also introduce these new people around to make sure everyone meets and greets the new people. Do this over a period of one month. It works and makes a new member feel so much more at home. Never take anything for granted!

Every group needs to have ensemble mentors: selected people who can and are willing to 'shepherd' new recruits into the ensemble family.

110 CHOIR/ORCHESTRA PERFORMANCE SCHEDULE

One of the great tools of music ministry is a listing of who sings what when (a.m. or p.m.) provided to each active choir, ensemble, instrumental group, handbell choir or praise team. This is wonderful way to keep your people up-to-date. Most who do this kind of ministry do it by semesters: January to May, June to August, and September to December. Yes, it takes some advance planning on the part of the minister of music or choir director. No, it is not in concrete, and yes, the schedule can be changed. Yes, it will allow your people to make specific plans to be present when they feel then need to be present, and can allow them to miss when it is not absolutely necessary they be present. This is a good tool.

111 FIVE THOUGHTS CONCERNING CHOIR MEMBERS

1. Choir members are willing to pray or bring a short devotional, if asked in advance.

2. Life is too short to be involved in a dull rehearsal.

3. Changing seating often is a good to keep members from 'settling in'.

4. Refreshments are always nice, and not just for special occasions.

5. Once a semester put a clean sheet of paper on each choir member's chair. Let them write the director a note, no holds barred. Signing one's name is optional. The director will learn volumes.

112 FOUR THINGS EVERY CHOIR MEMBER SHOULD KNOW

1

Keep negative comments to yourself. There's no good reason to downgrade anyone or any section or the director or your pastor or your church. Always speak positively about your situation, even if you have to stretch it a bit.

2

Know your director's birthday and a lot more. Make sure your director is appreciated with the little things, such as cookies on the directors stand every once in a while — with no identification as to who put them there, or a sweat towel once every two months, or a half of a bunt cake, or seats to the symphony, or a bunch of 'love' notes from the choir members, or a birthday card shower, where your director receives many, many, many birthday cards from the choir members. Remember, a bit of appreciation goes a l - o - n - g way!

3

Keep your folder clean. Don't let garbage collect in that folder from week to week. Throw away all bulletins earlier than 1989. Get rid of gum and candy wrappers that make noise. (Well, save a couple for those boring service times when a bit of noise can be a welcome relief to the preaching.) Rid thyself of written notes that may get you in trouble sooner or later. Wash the hankies that have been there since 1977. Let's not start another epidemic!

4

Be on the lookout for persons who might be interested in joining the choir or orchestra! The best prospects come from within the church family.

113 FIVE THINGS EVERY CHOIR MEMBER SHOULD KNOW

Have a red pencil ready to properly mark the music with your director's comments and suggestions. Spell as correctly as possible. *(Crescendo* is NOT spelled 'kirsendough'.)

____

A

Always be on time, or ahead of time. There is never an excuse, barring emergency, for anyone to be late for choir rehearsal.

____

B

Know which tenor to whom you can point when you make an obvious error in singing a particularly difficult phrase.

____

C

Don't talk during rehearsals, except about musical things! It is frustrating to the conductor to have conversations going on while he or she is trying to rehearse another section. Common courtesy applies here.

____

D

Look for surprises under your choir chair from time to time! You may find a candy bar, a CD, a picture of your college roommate, or a ticket to the movie. If you don't find anything – ever – complain to your director, or the President (your choir president, not Bush).

____

E

114 FIVE COMEDIC THINGS EVERY CHOIR MEMBER SHOULD KNOW

When you drop your hymnal and the pastor turns to look at who's making all that noise, always point to one of the basses!

____

1

Always carry an extra can of Tenor Mace to help keep the tenors in line!

____

2

Don't believe the rumor that choir robes were made to hang sideways or upside down!

____

3

MORE

If you must eat doughnuts in the loft on Sunday morning following the anthem, get the ones that don't spew custard when you bite into them!

4

Don't have the same person come to the choir loft door and motion to you to come to the phone following the anthem. It will begin to get obvious why you are leaving! (Why are you always leaving?)

5

115 FIVE MOSTLY SERIOUS THINGS EVERY CHOIR MEMBER SHOULD KNOW

1 It's really helpful to let your director know when you will absent from a rehearsal or service. It helps him or her plan better. Believe it or not, you *are* important.

2 Help build spirit in your vocal section by being affirming, kind, helpful, and the one who makes sure everyone knows everyone, even the tenors.

3 Proclaim 'National Tenor Day' the next rehearsal and require everyone to be nice to all tenors, whether they want to or not! Bring lots of cheap gifts for the tenors.

4 Always have the right music, in order, in your folder, in advance. Don't wait till rehearsal begins and then complain because you don't have everything necessary.

5 Affirm your minister of music often. A note of thanks, a small expression of gratitude, such as cookies, bunt cake or ice cream coupons will do wonders for his or her spirit!

116 FOUR THINGS EVERY CHOIR MEMBER SHOULD *REALLY* KNOW

1 Have a red pencil ready for properly marking of music from the director's comments and suggestions. Spell as correctly as possible. (*Crescendo is* NOT spelled 'kirsendough'.)

2 Always be on time, or ahead of time. There is never an excuse, barring emergency, for anyone to be late for choir rehearsal or performance.

3 Know which tenor to whom you can point to and blame when you make an obvious error in singing a particular difficult phrase.

4 Don't talk during rehearsals, except about musical things! It is frustrating to the conductor to have conversations going on while he is trying to rehearse another section. Common courtesy applies here.

117 GETTING TO KNOW YOU

One of the continuing frustrations of ministers of music is finding creative and innovative ways of allowing the choir members to get to know each other on a more personal and first-name basis while still have time for rehearsal. Remember: the choir room can be one of, if not the most, intimidating places in the church!

Here are some suggestions that you may find worthy of consideration:

NAMETAGS, WITH A LARGE FIRST NAME AND VOICE PART INCLUDED. Easy to read and useable over several weeks, this is always a help. Prepare the nametags and place them on a board. Ask the members to pick up their nametags and wear them in rehearsal; this also can serve as their attendance record. Remind them to put the tags back for the next rehearsal.

RECOGNIZE TWO CHOIR MEMBERS PER REHEARSAL. Have the chosen two stand, introduce themselves by telling certain things: name, where they live, what they do (school, job, etc.), favorite dog/cat, food, car (if they could afford it), color, and anything else that would give insight into this person. Those two people should also get to sit in 'special' chairs, such as a soft-seated chair or decorated chair.

MYSTERY CHOIR MEMBER. Select one person per week and post clues around the choir room, in chairs, on walls, in the music, as to the identity of this person. The first choir/ensemble member to guess the identity the mystery choir member is — even if it is in the middle of a song — wins a CD!

APPOINT ONE PERSON IN EACH SECTION to make sure everyone in that section knows all the names of those in the section! Give 4 minutes during rehearsal for these persons to allow people to call each other's names.

COSTUME ONE OR TWO PERSONS PER WEEK, with a real costume or simply a choir robe, and everyone gets to ask this person questions during the entire rehearsal time, as time allows! The costumed person is the 'person of the week'. Use seasonal themes as costume ideas.

These are for starters! You can be as creative as you wish to be! Go for it!

118 NOTES OF AFFIRMATION

There just isn't enough affirmation going on these days!

Everyone is running here and there, busy, involved, too many things to get done, so little time to do them, and not many people are thinking about affirming someone! But you can do it easily!

Before Wednesday night's choir rehearsal, write 4 or 5 notes of affirmation to certain members and place these hand-written notes on their choir chairs or taped to the back of the chair. When the choir member comes in, finds the note, opens and reads it, a smile of joy will certainly come across his or her face! Make sure that, over a period of time, every member of your choir gets an affirmation note (be sure to keep some kind of list and check it off so that no one is overlooked). This is a grand way to begin the new choir year!

119 MOVE 'EM OUT AND AROUND

Move the choir members around often in rehearsals!

Don't allow the choir members to become married to a special seat or spot in the choir room where they think they can put down roots and stay forever! Moving the choir members around will allow you to hear the balance from different setups. A good way to excite the choir is to put them in quartets or double quartets and let them sing with other voice parts near by. This will challenge their musicianship and make them listen more carefully to parts. Sure, it might take a bit of time, but it will be worth it in the end.

Remember: don't sing with the choir, or even mouth words! They have the music in front of them and mouthing the words doesn't help one bit. Singing with your choir keeps you from hearing the blend, balance or errors!

120 PENCILS...A MUST

All choir and orchestra members should be required to have pencils! How can a director conduct a rehearsal without seeing that his or her people have their own pencils, preferably red pencils!?!? There is an old Chinese Proverb: "He who hath not marked score sing solo at wrong time!"

Members should be trained weekly to mark their own scores carefully so the director doesn't have to teach the same thing week after week! The marked score will save valuable minutes. I remember when I was a minister of music in Atlanta, telling my sopranos to *"crescendo!"* Write it out, I told them, so you won't forget. Later that month, I was collecting the scores and one of the sopranos had written 'kirsendough.' That was *'crescendo'* to her! More power to the written word. I didn't care how she spelled it as long as she did it!

Encourage your people to mark the music carefully and you'll find rehearsals will go smoother, and you won't be repeating yourself so often! Remember: everyone needs to have their own music in rehearsal, and they need to be allowed to mark in their music. Ultimately, it will pay off, I assure you!

121 TAKE AUGUST OFF

That's right! Give your adult choir the whole month of August off. This allows time to do the 5 R's:

Refresh
Relax
Renew
Re-energize
Rest

They would be off from rehearsal nights only, of course, and would still sing on Sunday mornings, as usual. They could sing old favorites, standards, and sugar-sticks with only10 minutes of rehearsal done early on Sunday.

Begin the big push for choir enrollment the Wednesday after Labor Day. The choir members should, by the way, re-enroll each year, to 'clean the rolls', as someone used to say. Make the choir members feel the responsibility to register and begin again. You will find this a wonderful beginning for the new choir year. I guarantee it will work...trust me here!

122 TAKE A WEEK OFF

The choirs and orchestra have worked very hard preparing for the Christmas, Palm Sunday and Easter Sunday music and/or production.

Have they been faithful? Yes!

Have they been supportive? Yes!

Are they tired? You bet they are!

Give them the next week off, completely, and tell them not to come to rehearsal, but to enjoy a free evening with their families. Then, the next week, when they show up for rehearsal, have the room decorated, have homemade ice cream available with coffee, water or soft drinks. If this is not available, have cookies and cake, or something to express your appreciation for their hard work! Don't let the opportunity pass to express your feelings to those who work so hard for the Lord, and for you, on a weekly basis!

123 TEN WAYS TO IRRITATE THE CONDUCTOR

by Elf Ehly, noted Missouri choral conductor, clinician, teacher, mentor, and musician

1. Never show a pleasant expression on your face while singing. Music is a 'serious' business.
2. Chew on the words and rush the diphthongs. This is especially true in country music.
3. Pretend your neighbor's vowel is a disease. Do not conform to it.
4. Hide your age. Make your tone quality sound much more immature than your age.
5. Don't be a 'middle of the roader'. Sing either louder or softer than everyone else.
6. Never tune your voice to other singers. You cannot trust them. Besides, tuning is reserved for instrumentalists!
7. Never conform to another's interpretation. Strive to be independent and pursue your own interpretation.
8. Take noisy breaths so the conductor will be sure you know where to breath.
9. Give visible proof of your breathing by heaving the chest in a rise and fall motion when you inhale and exhale.
10. Form the vowel to about ½ of its potential shape. This saves lip and tongue energy.

124 TEN WAYS TO IRRITATE YOUR SINGERS *by Elf Ehly*

1. *Prepare the singers for the downbeat, then raise your baton and talk, talk, talk!*
2. *Keep your head in the score while lecturing the singers for not 'watching' the director.*
3. *Insist on detail and perfection, but never give suggestions. After all, you are the conductor!*
4. *Shout directions to them while they are singing. Tell them to write notes for bar 10 while they are singing bars 15 through 20.*

5
Sing along with the sections, loud and clear, so you won't have to hear all their wrong notes.

6
Assume everyone is singing out of tune on purpose and don't try to fix it.

7
Insist on finesse, especially while you are conducting in large, broad, sweeping motions.

8
Don't ever give explanations or suggestions. The singers/accompanists should learn to read your mind.

9
Keep them guessing as to where you wish to begin. A befuddled mind is an active mind!

10
Never smile at the choir while they are singing, for music is work!

125 THINGS ALL CHOIR MEMBERS SHOULD KNOW

When someone departs the choir loft early, take the next opportunity to move in and fill that place. It looks foolish to have a choir of 40 with 5 big holes spread out in the loft. Fill in the spaces!

If unsure, always ask the question…if it's about music.

Basses date altos, but usually marry sopranos.

Choir members should have a sense of accomplishment after each rehearsal, so make sure you accomplish something. This can be the introduction of a wonderful new anthem, chasing the final notes on a well-rehearsed one, or just letting them have a performance schedule. They look to you for leadership. Provide it!

MORE

Mark upcoming events on the calendar as far ahead as you can to avoid conflicts.

Be an encourager of the director, accompanist, and others around you.

Talk little… sing a lot.

Make sure that, at some point in rehearsal, someone is recognized for some accomplishment. It helps to inform others and honors the one being recognized.

It isn't true that just because the point on your pencil is broken, you are excused from writing cues or comments in your score. Get a fresh pencil!

126 WHAT ARE YOU DOING THAT SOMEONE COULD DO FOR YOU?

Many music ministers thrive on doing everything by themselves, with no outside help. They set up chairs. They take down chairs. They move chairs around. They take chairs to the choir loft. They take chairs from the choir loft. They straighten choir room chairs. They go get chairs. They take chairs back.

The 'chairs' idea is my entry into the fact that much of what we do in music ministry can be given away to others who are standing on the sidelines, watching and waiting to be asked to get involved. We should be training people in all aspects of leadership, from the most difficult to the most simple, like moving chairs.

Doing everything by yourself and never asking for help is a sure sign of insecurity, a lack of trust in other people, and the thinking that no one can do it better than you can do it. Well, they can, and will, if asked!

Worship and Worship Planning

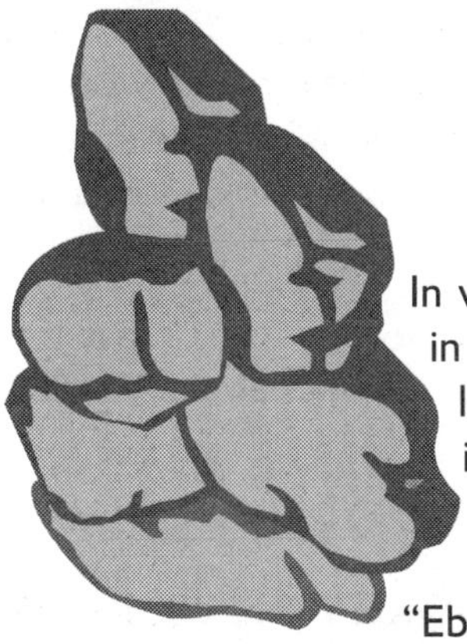

127

by Rob Hobby **BUILDING YOUR OWN "EBENEZER"**

In worship planning recently, God gave me a real jewel that I used in our Sunday service and it blest and taught our people a powerful lesson. I had chosen the hymn, "Come, Thou Fount of Every Blessing," as a part of our worship medley. As I read the text, my heart was drawn to the words, "Here I raise mine Ebenezer, hither by Thy help I'm come." The idea God gave me was to build an "Ebenezer" during the praise/worship music segment of the service. Prior to the service, I collected four large rocks, and enlisted three volunteers to join me in placing the stones on our platform. I used the hymn as a part of a D-major praise medley that included: "We Bring the Sacrifice of Praise," "Come Thou Fount" (Sacred Harp Tune), and "As the Deer."

After singing "Come Thou Fount," I spent a couple of minutes explaining the meaning of "Ebenezer" as "stone of help" from the Biblical account in I Samuel. I related these events for the Israelites to spiritual markers in our own lives. I instructed our people for the next few moments to remember spiritual markers in their own lives, and to thank God for what these events have meant to them. As the piano continued a soft segue from "Come Thou Fount" to "As the Deer," I went first and placed a large rock, here-to-fore unseen by the congregation, on the top step up to our platform, remaining on my knees briefly in prayer. I was followed in succession by a deacon, a choir member, and an eleven-year-old child, each adding their stone to create a monument effect. With this powerful symbol in place, we concluded the segment with "As the Deer" and the morning prayer led by our pastor, who, by the way, was almost too emotional to lead the prayer. I had not told him about it earlier as I wanted him to experience the same effect as the other worshipers.

I know that we should not always judge worship by outward emotion, but historically, our congregation is not very high on the emotional scale. However, after this part of the service, there were few dry eyes in the house. God had used a simple pile of rocks to create a powerful spiritual illustration, and we are a stronger church for it. I highly recommend this simple exercise if one is seeking to use new and innovative ways to lead God's people to His throne.

128

HOW LONG HAS IT BEEN?

Be honest now and think it over before you speak. Here is the question of the day:

How long has it been since you really changed the order of worship in your church?

Careful now! Changing the order of worship is more

MORE

than changing the titles of the hymns, or the sermon title (if there is one), or the anthem, or the solo, and so forth. Of course, you probably do that! I'm talking about really thinking through your order of worship and making changes that will allow your people to be better worshipers, to have a better communication with the Father, to allow time for celebration and quiet, for joy in His presence and time with each other. Changing the order of worship requires thinking, time, meditation, creativity, good planning, and a bit of the 'unknown'. Changing the order of worship is more than moving the Doxology around! It is more than moving the anthem around.

I encourage you to give some special time to creative thinking as to how you can change the order of worship in your church to meet better the worship needs of your people. You will be amazed at their response.

129 PRIORITY ON WORSHIP

by the religion researcher George Barna

Five requirements for a church to place a priority on worship:

1. Leaders in the church must demand that we engage in true worship.
2. People in the church must refuse to accept empty worship events. They have to hold their leaders to higher standards.
3. Establish 'worship experience' as a benchmark of Christian development, rather than worship service attendance.
4. Be open to being a bit uncomfortable in worship, allowing spontaneity, allowing the senses to be flooded, allowing God to interact with us. We're communicating with an amazing God.
5. Recognizing true worship is a key to church growth and church health. Two things allow a church to grow: (1) relationships between people on the outside and people on the inside, and, (2) a relationship with God through a regular connection with God.

130 WHAT CAN BRING A FRESH ENCOUNTER TO THE WORSHIP EXPERIENCE?

Every church musician, be they in small, medium or large-sized churches, must be willing to rethink worship planning – often! Here are eight suggestions to assist in this process:

A

Be open to new ideas and concepts. Don't be afraid to experiment.

B

Use your own ideas. Your creativity can enhance a worship service.

C

Use ideas and suggestions from laypeople who are concerned and interested in worship.

D

Always search the scriptures for themes, concepts, and inspiration.

E

Friends in the music ministry can be a big help. Find out what your friends are doing and if their ideas are usable in your situation.

F

Attend as many conferences as your schedule will allow. Never think that you know it all and can't learn anything new! Never be intimidated by thinking you should not attend a conference, whatever the reason! If you need what the conference offers, go!

G

Read, read, and read some more about worship. There is a lot of material available, be on the lookout.

H

If you are unwilling to continually better your music ministry…give it up!

131 AMERICAN BANDSTAND VERSUS MTV

I loved Leonard Sweet's statement in his book, *Soul Tsunami:*

> "We are attempting to do an 'American Bandstand' church in an 'MTV' world."

Wow, what insight. He also says (hang on here!) that: "the church, as we know it, is dead. Long live the church!" Sweet makes a wonderful point that one of the main features of the church of the 21st century will be the arts, and he asks what we are doing in our churches to promote art, music, painting, photography, video, sculpture, dance, and much more. He says that the church should be promoting their own people who have gifts and skills in these areas, and giving them a platform. I heartily agree. How can we do this?

Summer is a marvelous time to attempt new and creative things. How about having:

A Sunday-night musicale,

featuring music written, composed, arranged and performed by members of your church. You'll be astounded by how many composers and lyricists you will find in your membership if they know their work will get a hearing. Include good poetry in this venue, too.

An evening of viewing art works

created by members: paintings, sculptures, and such, put on display for the membership to peruse and (perhaps) purchase.

An evening of drama

written, staged, and performed by members of your church. There are a lot of would-be actors and actresses in your church who are anxious to have a performance opportunity.

A Sunday-night viewing

of photographs taken by members of your church, perhaps on a certain theme. You'll be surprised how many photographers you have in your membership, who do a very good job and would like people to see their work.

A professional video

of several events in your church, including some of the worship services, choir rehearsals, meetings, fun activities, nursery, children/youth areas, with good questions and responses. Have a Sunday night where this church-related video is shown on a big screen with good projector. It will be an instant hit.

Technology

132 EMAIL ETIQUETTE

Email is the powerful new tool of this age, and knowing how to use it effectively is becoming increasingly important. Other than the phone, email is the most efficient way of quick and easy communication, and email is probably cheaper than the phone. Like a poorly written business letter, a poorly written email can lessen your credibility.

Here are some hints for better email etiquette:

Signature Always sign your email message. Sometimes I receive an important email for a prayer request or big news but there is no name at the end, so I'm left guessing who sent it. If I don't recognize the address, and if I can't find out, I can't answer. Always sign your name.

Look professional Rarely is an email message best communicated using colors, images or cute type styles. I compare many of the messages I receive to sending an important business letter on colored notepaper with pictures of cats or butterflies in the margin. It just ain't done! And, many computers and different servers don't have the fonts and colors required and the email comes to the person looking bland or whompy-jawed! It's just not professional.

ALL CAPS? People sometimes send emails in ALL CAPS. It feels like I'm being YELLED AT the whole time I'm reading it! Caps mean EMPHASIS! Caps in an email are the way to YELL.

Grammar Some emails have poor grammar and punctuation. Even though email is a primary tool for quick communication, it reflects you and your personality just as much as a business letter. Take an extra moment to check spelling, grammar and punctuation.

Signature file Set up a signature file that is inserted at the end of every email you send. Every email program has a way to set up a brief description of who you are. You'll never forget to sign an email.

Attachments Attached files are a primary way for computer viruses to spread because they are designed to attach themselves to outgoing email. Make sure you know from whence a file comes before you send it on to someone else.

Forwarding If you pass along a joke or an inspiring story, take time to erase all the other sources from which it comes. I got a four-line story the other day that was 7 pages long due to all of the addresses of everyone who had previously sent the story. People are no longer bothering to read forwarded materials with lots and lots and lots of previous stuff. If you must pass on a story, erase all the other 'stuff'.

Check sources Check stories and prayer requests before forwarding them. The prayer request about "David" who is dying in China of intestinal virus was written three years ago. David is well, back in the states, but the email is still being sent around. The O'Hair story about the FCC wanting to stop religious broadcasting is 12 years old, and she didn't even submit that request to the government. A good rule of thumb: before you forward a prayer request or an emergency email, check it out first to make sure it is current. There are lots of things going around that are simply no longer valid.

Changing addresses When changing your email address, send both the old and the new address so we can delete the old as we add the new.

Respond promptly Answer email quickly. Usually when people send you an email, they are anxiously awaiting a response. Waiting 2-3 days is as slow as 'snail mail'.

133 THE INTERNET FEARS OF CHURCH LEADERS

Some laypersons are concerned that a staff member will spend more time online than in personal ministry – the 'high tech - low touch' fear. This is not 21st-century thinking! A staff member can be in touch with church members and get an assignment accomplished in less time than he or she could by snail mail or by phone! A responsible staff member knows to be in touch with the people and when to be online. Assuming the worst is a not a 21st-century outlook and will hinder technological ministry, which is the keystone of the future for the church.

Fearing that time at the computer will be wasted on games or the Internet and not spent on 'actual' church work is a common concern of some laypersons. How shortsighted this is. The future is now, and a responsible staff member who is committed to the Lord will balance computer and Internet time with church time. There is a trust factor that comes into play here – if the church fathers do not trust their staff members to do what God has called them to do, then both the church and the staff members will be in trouble down the road.

Don't delay! Get on the Internet and on email as soon as you can.

134 HOW IMPORTANT IS EMAIL?

"Help! My church has just put computers in the offices for staff, but the powers in the church won't allow us to hook up to an email service. Can you give some suggestions as to how we might persuade the church leadership to allow this to happen?"

"Our church has computers but we are not on the Internet. Why should we be hooked up? Is it difficult and how important is it to be online?"

These are just two of several emails received recently from church staff people, asking why they should be on line for email. Here are some reasons:

QUICK Email is the quickest, easiest, cheapest and most efficient means of communication available today, other than word of mouth. As we move into the 21st century, every household will soon have access to email; it will become even more important than it is today. It is the wave of future communication.

IMMEDIATE Email can put you in immediate touch with church members, committee members, choir members, staff members, and provide a source of 'instant' communication while you are online.

GROUPS Church staff can set up groups on email with whom they wish to communicate often. For instance, one can put the church choir in a separate group, and email the members before rehearsal or after rehearsal to inform the choir of emergency prayer requests, pass along special rehearsal reminders, and more. One can set up all committees in separate groupings and communicate with them more effectively and certainly cheaper than 'snail mail'.

CHEAP There are several free email services, including Juno and Hotmail. All you need is a modem and a phone line. It is best to have a dedicated phone line, a second line that is used just for Internet and fax, but you can use any phone line to access the Internet. Some services cost money. I'm partial to America Online (AOL) and for $23.95 per month, you can have unlimited time. For $9.95, you can get up to ten hours per week, and that is ample for most people.

FUTURE Church lay leadership should be pushing the staff to step into the 21st century, not holding them back by not allowing a connection to the Internet. Most lay people have up-to-date equipment in their offices, so why shouldn't the church staff have good equipment that makes it easier, more effective and faster to communicate with each other, with the church family and the world? There is a whole new world out there in Internet land and the church staff should have access to it for the good of the church and ministry.

RESOURCES The Internet provides a wealth of resources for the staff that can be of valuable assistance to the church. There are websites that will enhance all the ministries of the church and complement and help each ministry. To keep staff from visiting these websites and gaining valuable information is to hinder church growth for the future. The 21st century is now, and if you don't get into the flow you're only delaying the inevitable.

135 SIGNS OF THE TIMES

Recently, Esther and I took the interstate to our next destination. She was studying for her upcoming presentation so, while driving, I began to notice billboards. Specifically, I began to notice that the first eight billboards had either a website address or an email address. My interest peaked, and I found that during a 50 mile stretch, 95% of the billboards I saw had either website or email addresses! I thought back on several major magazines I had read last week, and the vast majority of them also have websites and/or email addresses in their advertisements.

Then, I began to think: If websites and email addresses are the wave of the future and are so predominant in our culture and society, then why is the church not in the forefront? I rarely receive a letter from a church that has an email or website address on their stationary. I began to wonder how many other churches did not have email connections, and why they might not have such.

I thought:

Does the leadership lack trust that the Internet will be used properly?

Does the leadership not want the staff to be able to communicate with the world outside the 'church fortress' and to learn new things?

Do they not have anyone with knowledge to set up and teach an Internet system in their church?

Are they fearful of what the staff will learn by having access to over 1 billion websites, many having religious or spiritual helps, guides, and studies?

Does the staff not have the ability or time to learn to work the Internet system?

This phenomenon is not going to go away! Technology is only going to get better and stronger, becoming even more accessible to the public and easier to use. Churches can no longer put their collective heads in the sand and wait till email and websites pass away.

How can the church utilize this technology?

Many churches are using their website and/or membership email addresses to send their weekly church paper, thereby saving money. You'll be amazed by how many members of your church have email in their homes!

Choir directors can get information, prayer requests, a weekly choir paper, and announcements to their choirs via email. One minister of music provides the weekly rehearsal schedule every Tuesday for his choir members on email. He has 90% of his choir members on email!

Information can be sent to visitors and new members if a place for email address is included on the visitor's form.

Church business could be provided, in advance, to the membership via email, informing the membership of what is taking place or has taken place, since attendance at these meetings is so small. Perhaps a way could be found to make email a voting resource for business meetings.

There is so much out there for us in technology that can be so useful to the local church and yet, many of our churches don't even have computers for their staff! One minister of music told me recently that he has had a computer in his office for one year, and it is not connected as yet. The leadership won't allow him to go online until everyone on staff has the same technology. I would say, "one is better than none!"

The church can no longer keep their heads in the sand on this technology issue!

136 THE TECHNOLOGICAL CHURCH

Twenty-Seven Possible Technological Scenarios of Activities for Staff and Office, by Gary Nichols, Associate, Discipleship Training Department, Florida Baptist Convention, Jacksonville, Florida

Monday morning, church office personnel go online to report to the local association and state convention offices the Sunday School attendance, decisions made during worship services, and other relative statistics. 1

2 Online prayer list is updated with requests, answered prayer and praises. (Note: some persons may ask that their prayer requests not be posted publicly.) People who access the site may email requests to be added.

Prayer requests are emailed to prayer partners/warriors/champions who will spend a significant portion of their time praying for the requests. This group includes retired persons, senior adults and others who do not work outside the home. 3

4 The church office emails, directly to a pager, a prayer to a person who has made a request for a specific time and purpose, like a prayer for an important business meeting or family issue. Access to this technology could send an email a few minutes prior to an appointment assuring the recipient of concern and including a prayer.

Guests who attended Sunday school and worship services are emailed an appreciation message. They can be asked to evaluate their Sunday school and/or worship experience using an online form, which is emailed back to the responsible person in the church office. It may be possible for this form to be returned anonymously. 5

6 Visitors to the church website who sign the guest book are emailed information and a map to the church. (Maps from one address to another, no matter the distance, are easily obtained on any search engine.)

7 Seems that everybody has a web page these days. Been thinking about building your own? It may be easier and cheaper than you imagined. The web is filled with sites designed to host and help you build your website – all free. Carving out your own corner of the web is only a few clicks away.

8 Technical personnel (tech crew) transfer worship and sermon video clips to the church web page. A digitally recorded 'welcome' video message by pastor or staff is updated. This message may be emailed to Sunday's visitors. A visitor to the website may be given the chance to download the entire worship service on digital video to be viewed on their home PC, off-line.

9 Photos of new members, taken with a digital camera, are posted on the website. (Remember: we should never assume that it is allowable to post personal information or photos on the web. Permission must be obtained.) Digital cameras can be purchased very inexpensively these days.

10 The pastor uses his or her personal church-office computer network email to communicate to appropriate staff members, such as minister of music and tech crew, new sermon topics or scriptures. (This may also be accomplished at home.)

11 Tech crew uses Christian web search engines to locate sources for appropriate video illustrations of topics and/or video depicting selected scriptures for upcoming weeks.

12 The minister of music searches Christian worship data banks on the web for related drama scripts or ideas for creative presentation of selected scripture passages. With adequate lead-time, he or she can look for suitable choral music through a variety of resources from publishers, music dealers, friends, MMEmail and more.

13 Church office personnel email Sunday-school teachers and outreach leadership information regarding Sunday's visitors.

14 Pastor uses online study helps in sermon preparation. He or she may download information into the sermon notes.

15 The minister of education uses search engines to locate and download web resources to assist leaders in preparing and presenting Sunday-school lessons and discipleship courses. That information is downloaded and emailed to leadership.

16 The minister of education uses a computerized registration system to track which members are involved in discipleship/small-group studies and ministries. This data is linked to a database of leadership and ministries needs, allowing him or her to match members' interests and talents with ministry opportunities and allowing for follow-up and promotion of future small-group studies.

17 The church office personnel use sophisticated desktop publishing software to layout the church newsletter using photo and clip-art galleries on CD-ROM or downloaded from the web, along with digital or scanned photos from church events.

18 In weekly staff meeting, all staff share information learned via emails, pagers, church web pages and contacts with real-live people. They know that information is useless, unless it becomes knowledge. Staff members use organizational software to plan ministry strategies and share this information in report form with all staff. If a staff member is away, he or she is included in the meeting via ICTV (unless they are on vacation or retreat, of course!).

Church staff uses database information to match members with ministry team opportunities for long-range or short-term projects or events. 19

20 The pastor, minister of music, instrumental leaders and tech crew meet to plan next month's Sunday worship services; they finalize plans for next Sunday. Planning includes use of computer-generated graphics, words to songs/hymns, thematic video, sermon outline/notes, microphone/sound system/audio needs, sound/lighting effects, choreograph video cameras and use of video/data projectors onto large screens, and perhaps, to overflow areas. Using information from worship attendee information cards, and entered into a database, they determine the demographics of the various worship services styles.

On Sunday, or any other time people come to the church for any activities, they may go to a computer screen and email prayer requests directly to the pulpit or tech booth or office, where requests are printed and passed on to worship leaders for immediate prayer. 21

22 Visitors are personally greeted and may be assisted in finding Sunday-school classes, etc., by the greeter using an interactive computer monitor for a virtual church tour. Most churches are not so large, though some are confusing enough to need this mapping system.

From interactive computer/video monitors located throughout church buildings, parents of preschoolers can look in on their children as the parents move from Sunday School to worship. 23

24 Parents of preschoolers are given pagers so they can easily be located while on the property if there is an emergency. This notification system is presently used in many churches.

Tech crew use digital cameras to put instant photos of new members on large screens in front of worship center. 25

26 Tech crew records the worship service onto a writable CD. A limited number of worship service videos on digital videodisk are available for purchase by the end of the service. Members may play these on their PCs, DVD drive or DVD player on their home entertainment system. (Digital video cameras sell for $800-$4500.)

Church staff use the church's computer lab at various times and days for workshops on: senior adults and email; families and the Internet; and homework. 27